SHERLO A
ROSET
MYSTERY

CW00687908

The Early Casebook of Sherlock Holmes

Book One

Linda Stratmann

SAPERE BOOKS

SHERLOCK HOLMES
AND THE
ROSETTA STONE MYSTERY

Published by Sapere Books.

20 Windermere Drive, Leeds, England, LS17 7UZ,
United Kingdom

saperebooks.com

ISBN: 978-1-80055-389-7

With all my good wishes to Don't Go into the Cellar Theatre Company *and the wonderful Jonathan Goodwin, the modern embodiment of Sherlock Holmes*

'…when you knew me first … I had already established a considerable, though not very lucrative connection. You can hardly realise then, how difficult I found it at first, and how long I had to wait before I succeeded in making any headway. When I first came up to London I had rooms in Montague Street, just round the corner from the British Museum, and there I waited, filling in my too abundant leisure time by studying all those branches of science which might make me more efficient. Now and again, cases came my way, principally through the introduction of old fellow students, for during my last years at the University there was a good deal of talk there about myself and my methods.'

Holmes speaking to Watson, in *The Musgrave Ritual*

From
Memoirs of a Medical Man
by A. Stamford FRCS

1924

INTRODUCTION

I first encountered Mr Sherlock Holmes in the spring of 1876. He was then undertaking some courses of study at St Bartholomew's Medical College and exciting a certain amount of attention amongst both students and teachers because of his unorthodox and undisciplined methods. He attended lectures and demonstrations, making copious notes, but was always a remote and solitary presence. He made a corner of the library his own, and also haunted the students' reading room, where he folded his body into an armchair and perused the periodicals with an intensity which discouraged conversation. It was not until I came to know him better that I understood that these were simply the outward appearances of the operation of a uniquely brilliant mind.

I was then engaged in my own studies leading to a general qualification in surgery. Some years earlier, as a youth of modest ambition, I was employed at St Bartholomew's — or Barts as it is commonly known — as a surgical dresser. I was working under the supervision of John Watson, a gentleman who impressed me with his diligence, courage, and sound common sense. It was he who turned to me one day and said, 'You know, Stamford, I rather think you have what it takes to become a surgeon.' He told me how to equip myself to enrol on a course, and I thanked him for his confidence, and promised that I would not fail him. Soon afterwards he left to continue his studies at the University of London where he took his MD in 1878 and later became rather better known.

In those days, students enjoyed few opportunities for recreation. Some of the Oxford and Cambridge men at Barts had formed sporting clubs. Despite my humbler origins, my ability as a medium pace bowler had admitted me to the cricketing fraternity, while Holmes, never a man for team sports, was reputed to be uncommonly effective in the boxing ring. Our paths rarely crossed.

My first meeting with Sherlock Holmes was sufficiently startling to make a lasting impression. Until that moment we had never spoken, and his reputation for being not merely eccentric but possibly unhinged had led me to avoid rather than seek out his company. All that was to change. It was late in the day and I was hurrying to deliver a paper, one to which I had devoted a great deal of labour, to Professor Platt, whose speciality was diseases of the eye. I chanced to be passing the dissecting room where unclaimed corpses were laid out for our study when I heard an unusual dull thumping noise coming from within. Wondering whether a casement had somehow been left open and was moving in the breeze, I opened the door and peered in.

The sight that met my eyes shocked me to a standstill. Two bodies were ready for the knife, one that of a poor fellow in his twenties who had died following surgery and another of an older man, for whom surgery had not come in time. Standing over them was a figure like the physical embodiment of death itself. Holmes was very tall, at least six feet in height, but so slender that he appeared even taller. His profile was highly distinctive, with a prominent nose like a hawk's beak, and a firm chin. If it is possible to read character in a face, my impression at that moment was one of a purposeful, determined, single-minded individual, never to be deflected from a goal once he had it in his sights.

But it was his actions which astounded me. He was grasping a stout stick in one hand and using it to belabour the corpse of the younger deceased. I was about to conclude that he really was insane as had been reputed, affected perhaps by the strain of long hours of study, but then on hearing the door, he paused in his actions and turned to face me. I was immediately struck by his pale features, intense stare and glittering eyes, but they were not the eyes of a madman. I was seeing the penetrating almost mesmerising gaze of an observer.

He straightened, and the few tendrils of dark hair that had been disturbed by his efforts were carefully smoothed back into place by long slim fingers. He smiled and beckoned me forward. 'Come in and see this!' he exclaimed. Perhaps it was the fact that I did not immediately back away in horror and run from the room, but actually dared enter to see what he was doing, which eventually led to his sharing some fragments of information about his work.

Holmes revealed that he was conducting an experiment to show whether or not it was possible to produce bruises on a corpse. This issue had apparently been of great importance in a recent criminal trial. He was therefore working with corpses of all ages and dimensions and assaulting them with a variety of implements. I saw a singlestick, a poker, a walking cane, a bamboo switch and a cudgel on the bench. He was also making copious notes and sketches of his results, with the intention of writing a monograph on the subject.

Eventually he introduced himself. He was my own age, just twenty-two, and had enrolled at Barts the previous autumn after coming down from university. When we shook hands, I found his grip remarkably and unexpectedly powerful. What other experiments he was engaged in were not discussed then, but the state of his hands told me a great deal. As every medical student knows, when a drop of blood is required in the laboratory, one's own fingers are the most convenient source, however it was clear that Holmes took this to excess, and his fingers were not only stained with ink and marked with chemical burns but dotted with small strips of plaster.

'I see you study chemistry as well as medicine,' I said.

'Chemistry and anatomy,' he corrected me. 'I do not undertake formal medical training. But I will not detain you further. I perceive that you are on your way to report to Professor Platt to deliver an important paper, and he does not like to be kept waiting.'

I took my leave and had actually reached the professor's department before I wondered how Holmes had deduced where I was bound and why, as I certainly had not mentioned it.

He was not an easy man to get to know, and perpetually mysterious in that no-one could ever learn to what end he was pursuing his varied and vigorous studies. It may seem naive of me not to have realised that Holmes' true intentions were to become a consulting detective, but he was the first of that profession, the first and the best, and I suppose my imagination did not stretch that far. Watson himself, as I later discovered when I read his memoirs, never guessed the truth, even after several weeks of their sharing lodgings. At the time, therefore, I concluded that Holmes was a gentleman of independent means who unlike so many idlers of this world, wished to acquire knowledge on any subject as the fancy took him, and addressed himself to the solution of problems as an exercise for his brain.

There were long periods when he worked in the laboratories from morning to night, and we occasionally discussed his experiments, but this was followed by weeks when he was never seen there. He often struck me as almost too scientific, a man without emotion or compassion, but not deliberately cruel. I sometimes wondered if he was capable of administering a rare poison to an acquaintance, just to test its effect, although he would also have tried it on himself just as readily. I would not say that we ever became intimate friends, but I felt privileged when he chose to share his thoughts with me.

It amuses me now to think that it was I who was responsible for introducing Holmes to Dr Watson, who became his great friend and recorder of so many of his adventures. At the time I was conscious only that I was helping two admirable gentlemen find accommodation within their means, but I felt obliged to warn Watson that though Holmes was a decent enough fellow, he was regarded by some as having some curious methods of study. And here I have a confession to make. After arranging for the two to meet I suddenly developed misgivings in case Watson should find sharing lodgings with a noted eccentric untenable, and like a coward I downplayed the extent of my association with Holmes. Watson recorded me as claiming that I only knew him to talk to in the laboratory, and I am sure I did say something of the sort. That was certainly the place where I most often encountered him. But it is not the whole of the story by any means.

Over the years I have often reflected on the character of Mr Sherlock Holmes and concluded that he was a man devoted solely to intellect and the art of reasoning. He was not, I eventually realised, entirely without emotion, but he always strove to ensure that it was never allowed to cloud his judgement.

The one thing that excited him was the solution of a problem, be it a crime, a trivial oddity or an advance in medicine, and the world should be grateful that he chose to apply his talents for the public good. Much of his work resulted in enormous benefits to mankind. Some of it saved lives and reputations, some brought comfort to individuals, some affected the whole of a great nation, but I often felt that to Holmes the result made no difference. It mattered nothing to him if the mystery was fresh and poignant or was thousands of years old.

The mystery was all.

CHAPTER ONE

As I look back on a life spent in the service of medicine, I realise that the most extraordinary tales I have to tell are those relating to my youthful association with Sherlock Holmes, when I saw him apply his unparalleled powers of deduction to apparently insoluble mysteries. Several of these incidents I was at the time obliged to promise never to reveal to a living soul, but with the passage of many years that embargo has been removed, and I can at last describe in detail the full facts of one of the most extraordinary and audacious crimes of our time.

When I next saw Holmes after our first meeting, he was engaged on one of his lengthy sessions in the chemistry laboratory. I had recently overheard some of the other students discussing him with laughs of derision. He had been seen in the Tottenham Court Road stopping to peer with interest into a trench being dug by some workmen repairing water pipes. He had then very carefully taken a sample of the exposed soil with a penknife and placed it in an envelope which he put in his pocket. The purpose of this action was unclear. I said nothing but could not help wondering what my fellow students might have said if they had seen Holmes in the dissecting room belabouring corpses.

'Holmes!' I exclaimed, as he held up a test tube and tapped it smartly with the nail of one finger. He gave a little hum of disappointment, replaced the tube on its rack, and made a careful note, then turned to me. 'I am sorry to trouble you,' I said, 'I can see you are occupied.'

'Not at all,' he replied. 'I have reached an impasse to which I must devote some thought before I continue. The solution will have to wait for another day.'

Emboldened, I went on. 'The thing I wanted to ask was — I was curious to know how you knew where I was going the other day and why.'

A flicker of amusement passed over his face. 'The delivery of the paper? That was simple enough. Professor Platt lectures on diseases of the eye, and there was a monograph of his in your pocket. You were holding a portfolio of papers in a manner which suggested to me that its contents were of some importance to you. Your right cuff showed signs that you had undertaken a great deal of writing recently, and there were stains of ink which looked fresh showing that you had refilled your pen quite hurriedly more than once. I deduced the delivery of a completed paper.'

'Ah,' I said, 'yes, that seems obvious now that you explain it.'

'It is a question of observation and then employing those observations to make deductions. You have shown some ability in that yourself, when you assumed from looking at my hands that I pursued courses in chemistry and medicine.'

'I was wrong about the medicine.'

'You were. Some deductions can be made with a measure of certainty. Others, only with a degree of probability. For example, I venture to deduce that you have paid a visit to your parents recently.'

I stared at him and he laughed at my expression.

'You are right, of course, but —'

'The fountain pen in your pocket is of a kind often bestowed as a gift to students starting a new course of study by proud parents. When I last saw you, it was much finger marked by your recent labours. Since then, you have polished it. That provided one clue, and your recent visit to the barber completed the picture.'

I was about to comment on this when there was the sound of hurrying footsteps in the corridor. The door opened and a young man entered who was unknown to me. He was about my own age, smartly dressed but clearly in the grip of some strong emotion. There was an agitated pinkness about his cheeks and his blue eyes were bright with anxiety.

'Holmes,' he exclaimed, 'I am glad to have found you, I was told you might be here!'

I sensed that I might be wise to withdraw and made my excuses, saying that I had a paper by Professor Platt to peruse, but to my surprise the new arrival gave a little gasp at the name.

'Platt the eminent eye surgeon? You are a student of his?'

'Yes, he lectures here.'

'Then if you wouldn't mind the imposition, I would take it as a very great favour if you could remain to listen to what I have to say.'

I was understandably startled by this but agreed to his request.

The usual introductions were made, and I learned that the new arrival was called George Luckhurst and he had formerly been at college with Holmes.

Holmes had put aside his work and was studying his friend's features intently. 'I assume,' he said, 'that you have sought me out because of some singular difficulty concerning your uncle? Something you have only discovered on seeing him today?'

Luckhurst nodded. 'I hardly know where to begin. As you have rightly guessed —' I saw Holmes' eyebrows rise a little at this last word, but he did not interrupt — 'I came down to London today to pay one of my regular visits to my uncle not expecting that anything might be the matter.' Luckhurst turned to me, explaining, 'He is Dr Edgar Martinson, and he has for many years been a resident keeper at the British Museum, with particular responsibility for the Egyptian galleries. After the death of my parents twelve years ago he became as a second father to me.' Turning back to Holmes he continued, 'I called on him at his rooms today with the intention that we would take luncheon together. I noticed when we spoke that he seemed somewhat preoccupied and when I enquired after his health, he informed me that he had been slightly indisposed of late but was considerably improved. I thought to raise his spirits with an interesting tale, so I told him of that incident in your last term, Holmes, when you solved the mystery of the missing cummerbund. He listened to me very closely and seriously, and then he said that he would very much like to meet you. It was obvious to me from the way he spoke, that he had a pressing reason of his own to consult you. I asked him what the matter was, and after a moment of prevarication he at last admitted the truth. As far as he knows he is in good health; the mention of an indisposition was merely a story to divert me from his real concerns. He did however state that what he was about to tell me was in the strictest confidence. I am only revealing this to you on his authority and on the understanding that you will honour that confidence.'

We both earnestly reassured Luckhurst on that point and he proceeded.

'My uncle told me that he has recently seen strange appearances in the museum after dusk, at a time when all the visitors have gone. No-one should be there, but he declares that he has seen actual moving figures and a mysterious light. He naturally reported this to the attendants and careful searches were made, but as far as can be seen nothing at all is missing, or damaged or disturbed in any way. There is no sign of any intruder. But he is afraid, Mr Holmes, afraid for the safety of the museum where he has spent so much of his life and the precious objects it contains, afraid, I am sure, although he would not admit it, for himself, his own health. I begged him to see a doctor. He refused outright. Then I thought of an oculist, and I suggested Professor Platt. I have heard good things of him from an acquaintance of mine in connection with his work at the London Ophthalmic Hospital, but he refused that also. He protests that he has important work on hand which cannot be delayed.'

'Is your uncle afraid that a medical man would prescribe a rest from work?' I asked.

'I believe that might be the case. But that did make me think — what if it was the work itself which produced these visions?'

'Indeed,' said Holmes. 'But let us go at once to Dr Martinson and see what we can learn.'

Before I knew it, Luckhurst had thanked us effusively and hurried away to summon a four-wheeler and we followed him from the building. On the way, Holmes admitted to me without a trace of diffidence that he had long been in the habit of developing his powers of observation and deduction. While at university he had occasionally employed these abilities to solve some trivial mysteries presented to him by his fellow students.

'All too often,' he said with a little sigh that spoke of past disappointments, 'the mystery has been a commonplace affair, the solution easily visible to the meanest intelligence, but sometimes,' he added with a little tilt of his noble head and a gleam in his eye, 'there is a touch of the extraordinary, the outré which engages and stimulates the mind.'

'Do you think this is such a mystery?' I asked.

'One can always hope,' he said.

The four-wheeler drew up and as we climbed aboard, I realised that sympathetic as I was to George Luckhurst's obvious distress I could not repress a little thrill of anticipation that some interesting adventure lay ahead of me. How interesting and how dangerous it would turn out to be, I could never have guessed.

CHAPTER TWO

It was, I recall, a bright fresh day in the late spring, that time at the turn of the seasons when we bid farewell to winter mists and look forward to kinder weather. It may seem strange that I noted that at the time, but I believe that in my excitement my senses had become sharper, keener, and I observed more. London, as we rattled along the busy commercial and legal thoroughfare of High Holborn, unrolled before my eyes like a beautiful landscape, and displayed itself proudly as a place of industry and opportunity second to none.

Quelling my exuberant thoughts, I glanced at Holmes, who was studying our companion attentively. Luckhurst took no cheer from either the brilliant panorama or the weather, and I could see that his mind was engaged solely by concern for his uncle. There was a flower bud in his buttonhole, which must have been fresh that morning but was now rather knocked sideways and drooping somewhat like the despondent wearer.

'What is your subject of study, Mr Luckhurst?' I asked, mainly to encourage him to talk, as I hoped to enliven his mood.

'Classics,' said Luckhurst, after a moment in which he summoned up the energy for conversation, 'language, literature, art and history. Once I have taken my degree I hope to travel and teach. I am a great devotee of the marbles of the Greeks and Romans. My uncle's preference is for Egypt, but there is something about the ancient Egyptians and their obsession with death that always makes me a little nervous,' he added with a slight shudder. 'Classical art on the other hand, with its depiction of vigour and health, bodily beauty, youthful athleticism, is far more palatable.'

'Is your uncle a very noted expert on the Egyptians?' I asked.

'He is. It is his passion and has been since his youth. Are you at all familiar with the antiquities of Egypt?' he added, not very hopefully.

I was obliged to confess to an almost complete ignorance on the subject, adding that to my shame I had never visited the British Museum.

Holmes smiled a little. 'I frequently make use of the library, but I have never yet studied the antiquities or natural history of any country. I have not so far visited the galleries.'

Luckhurst paused awhile before he went on. 'My uncle,' he continued, 'and I wish to make this very plain, is not a man given to idle fancies. He is abstemious, devout, and very orderly and regular in his habits. He lives alone apart from an elderly manservant, Greenleaf, who has been with our family for many years, but he has many close acquaintances who share his interests and is respected and well-liked.'

'Is he a bachelor or a widower?' asked Holmes.

'He has never married, although I believe that he was once engaged to a young lady of good family, but it was broken off. I don't know why. It would have been an ideal match, too. They met in Egypt where she was assisting her brother on an excavation.'

Holmes was thoughtful. 'This does not weigh on his mind? Disappointed love can result in illogical behaviour.' His tone suggested that he was a stranger to both afflictions.

'I'm not sure. He never speaks of it. I only know because I once heard my great-aunt mention it. I think it happened long ago. No, what I am afraid of is that he is suffering from a disorder of the nerves brought about by overwork. Either that or this is the first sign of a disease of the eyes which requires attention or at the very least, a protracted period of rest.'

'I regret that these are both areas in which I cannot advise you,' said Holmes.

I very nearly added that I too was no great authority on either but decided to say nothing in case it jeopardised my participation. I resolved to learn as much as I could about Dr Martinson's condition, after which I might, if necessary, privately ask the advice of more senior men.

'The fact is, Holmes,' said Luckhurst plaintively, 'that you are the only man he has agreed to consult, and your powers of perception might well serve at least to eliminate the less probable explanations leaving only those which it would be wise for me to pursue.'

'That is a highly commendable approach,' said Holmes.

'And you, Mr Stamford,' said Luckhurst, 'I am so sorry to impose on you on such a slight acquaintance, but on learning that you were a student of Professor Platt — well, it occurred to me that had I introduced my uncle to a much older gentleman he might have suspected that I was bringing him a medical consultant against his explicit instructions, and refused to have anything to do with him, whereas...' he broke off with an expression of embarrassment.

I was rather touched by his concern and made some reassuring comments to the effect that I understood the difficulty of his position and would do what I could.

We alighted in Great Russell Street opposite the iron gates that led to the great quadrangle in front of the main building. The museum is well known to Londoners and visitors; indeed, it must be famous throughout the world, and I had both passed by it and seen it portrayed in the illustrated newspapers. Nothing, however, had fully prepared me for a closer approach to the giant portico, the double row of enormous columns, their massy width and dizzying height, like the entrance to a Greek temple. I had expected, indeed hoped, that we would mount the flight of wide stone steps leading to the colonnade and thus find myself stopping to wonder at it towering above me, but instead Luckhurst beckoned us to follow him as he crossed the quadrangle to a side wing of the great building.

'As one of the senior keepers my uncle has rooms here,' he explained. He knocked at the front door and we were admitted by a porter who clearly recognised Luckhurst and readily allowed us into an entrance hall.

We proceeded down a corridor reaching a door with a brass plate engraved 'E. Martinson' where Luckhurst knocked. It was opened after about a minute by a dignified looking man with white hair.

'Ah, Greenleaf,' said Luckhurst, 'I have brought Mr Holmes to see my uncle as requested and also Mr Stamford, a fellow student.'

The servant gave a courteous bow and invited us in. As he conducted us to a door, I could not help noticing that though he appeared sturdy for his age which I estimated as about sixty, that he walked with a slight limp, which slowed his movement. He knocked at the door with great care and solemnity. I guessed that Dr Martinson, given the nature of his profession, was a studious gentleman who appreciated receiving a gentle warning of visitors. I heard a voice asking us to enter, and Greenleaf opened the door, ushered us forward, and made the introductions before leaving.

Dr Martinson was a gentleman of about forty-five, lean and spare, very sombrely dressed in plain dark clothes. The only unusual thing about his appearance was that despite the warmth of the day, he wore gloves of very thin black leather. I wondered if this was something to do with his work in examining ancient materials. I was particularly interested to see what I took to be one end of a set of gold-rimmed reading spectacles protruding from his top pocket.

'Please do come in, gentlemen,' he said, in a friendly manner. The room we entered served as both sitting room and study. I saw Holmes looking about him with interest. It was large well-appointed and comfortably furnished, an apartment which any young student would envy. My own lodgings at the time were far smaller and more austere, and I guessed that Holmes was similarly situated.

The room was well provided with bookshelves which were filled with leather-bound volumes, and a desk was equipped with writing paper, pens, ink and a blotter. A large paper scroll lay in the centre of the desk and beside it a handheld magnifying glass.

The thing that really commanded my attention however was a large framed engraving on the wall, which despite my sparse knowledge I immediately recognised from the style of the illustration as a copy of an ancient Egyptian subject. On the extreme left of the picture two figures were outlined in profile, in the characteristic stiff formal manner, the purpose of which has always eluded me. One was clearly a man wearing a tall hat, the other rather smaller, a boy, bareheaded, and quite bald apart from a single long lock of hair. Both were carrying objects I could not identify. Stretching from these figures to the other edge of the engraving was what I can only describe as rows and columns of pictures and symbols. I could not begin to imagine what they might mean.

'How very extraordinary,' exclaimed Holmes, going to study the picture.

I saw Martinson's face soften to a smile. 'Ah yes, Mr Holmes, it is quite wonderful, is it not? This drawing is copied from a sculpture which was discovered quite recently at the temple of Osiris in Abydos. It is the most extensive list we have to date of the names of the pharaohs. I don't know if you have studied Egyptology at all?' he added.

'I regret I have not, but I am happy to be educated,' said Holmes.

Martinson took on this task with enthusiasm. 'Well, this large figure on the left is Pharaoh Seti I, and the smaller is his son, the future Rameses II. They are taking offerings to a deity. The other figures listed here are past pharaohs come to do them homage. There are seventy-six named in all, although despite the fact that there are no obvious omissions, many scholars believe it is still not complete. There were others who ascended the throne and we know of them because they feature in sculptures and papyri. It is thought that they may not have been considered genuine incumbents and their omission is therefore deliberate. Where they fall in the order is yet to be determined and is the subject of much debate. One was actually said to be a woman. But there is one other who is the focus of my current work. He is mentioned nowhere, and yet there are clues which I am pursuing, to restore him to his proper place in history.' He took a deep breath and I felt sure that he was about to expand on this topic, then he smiled. 'But I digress as is my wont. Please do take a seat.'

Holmes settled himself comfortably in an armchair, stretching out his long legs. 'Luckhurst tells me that you wish to consult me concerning a mystery. I assume it is not to discover a missing pharaoh which may be rather out of my line.'

'Oh no, but it does concern the museum.' Martinson sat at his desk and took a few moments to tidy some already very tidy papers, then he raised his head and stared at us with a pained expression. 'Mr Holmes, I am not given to flights of imagination. Neither am I a partaker of intoxicating liquor. I say that because I have in view of recent events, been accused of it, which I have found most distressing.'

'Especially as you are one of the Society of Friends,' observed Holmes.

'Why, how did you know that?' said Martinson, startled.

'Not all the volumes on your bookshelves deal with Egyptology.'

'Ah, yes of course. Well, I wish to assure you that on the night I am about to describe I had enjoyed nothing stronger than my usual nourishing drink of hot cocoa. Dusk was approaching, and the public were being ushered from our doors. The attendants were preparing to secure the building before they, too, left. There is a corridor connecting the keepers' residences to the main body of the museum but that is always locked at night. Last week — in fact it was a week ago today —' I saw Holmes frown at this — 'I was taking a pleasant walk around the deserted galleries in the last of the fading light before returning to my rooms. I should mention that our galleries and reading rooms are lit only by daylight, that is why they are so well furnished with large windows, and we are obliged to close so early in the winter months. The museum does not permit gas or oil or candles for fear of fire.' As he said this, I saw his gloved hands clench a little.

'I was in the long Egyptian gallery on the ground floor, and not looking for anything in particular when all of a sudden, I heard a strange sound. It was not footsteps, as it might have been had there been an intruder. No, it was more like a shuffling, or a whispering, as if some material was being dragged along the floor. I held my breath, and as quietly as I could, concealed myself behind one of the larger sculptures, and waited and watched, and eventually a sight appeared before my eyes that —' he stopped and made a convulsive little gasp. 'You must believe me. It was a procession of dark figures. I don't know how many of then there were, but there must have been several, and I had the impression that they formed a double and not a single line. They were moving very slowly indeed, they seemed to glide rather than pace. And in the midst of them, there was a curious glow in the dark. The light was so soft and faint, that it showed me nothing of the moving figures apart from what seemed to me like formless black shapes. I had never seen anything quite like it before. It was not any kind of lantern with which I am familiar, or a lamp or a candle, and it hovered in the air. None of the dark shapes was near enough to grasp it by any natural means. I could not see how it was supported, but yet it moved, it moved at the pace of the figures. I was too shocked to speak. Too afraid. In fact, I stood there so quiet and still that I do not think these creatures, if creatures they were, even knew that I was there. You will think me a terrible coward, Mr Holmes, but all I could think of at that moment was to slip away before they noticed me and fetch some assistance.'

'You did not approach for a closer examination?' asked Holmes, although I could tell from his voice that he knew the answer.

'I — no, I dared not. I hurried from the gallery, to fetch one of the attendants, but I couldn't find one; it is a very large building to search, and it was possible that they might have all left by then. I thought it better not to cry out for help in case — well, I think you understand. You can imagine the trepidation I felt when I summoned up enough courage to return to the gallery, just to make sure that our precious antiquities were unharmed. By then it was almost completely dark. The night sky was clear and there was just the barest of light through the windows from starlight, and a crescent moon. But there was nothing to see. Whatever vision had passed before my eyes had gone. And I hesitate to say it, Mr Holmes, but to my mind, what I had seen was nothing more or less than an ancient funeral rite, a procession of solemn priests paying homage to their dead pharaoh.'

CHAPTER THREE

Luckhurst had obviously heard his uncle's account before, but I confess that on my first hearing, it gave me that little shiver of fear which is always produced by a good ghost story.

I glanced at Holmes, but he appeared unmoved. 'What did you do next?' he asked.

'There was nothing I could do immediately,' said Martinson. 'Everything seemed safe and secure, so I returned to my rooms and spent a very unhappy and restless night. Naturally the very first thing I did the following morning was to report what I had seen to Dr Birch. He is the keeper of Oriental Antiquities which includes the Egyptian collection, and together we examined the gallery in daylight.'

'And did you find any evidence of intruders?' asked Holmes. 'Footprints? Fingermarks? The remains of some burnt material? Anything they might have left or dropped?'

Martinson looked a little helpless at these demands. 'All I can tell you is that the attendants made a very thorough search, as did I and Dr Birch, but no. We found no evidence at all that anyone had been there. No suggestion of forced locks or broken windows anywhere in the museum. It was suggested that all I had witnessed was simply some visitors who had got lost, which does happen from time to time, but if that was the case why were they not asking for directions to the exit instead of creeping about? Why could I not hear their footsteps? And what was that strange floating light?'

I could see that Holmes' attention was directed towards more tangible matters than antique ghosts or creatures of the imagination. 'Do you have any reason to suspect that the museum might be the target of thieves or vandals?' he asked.

'It has been known,' said Martinson, sorrowfully. 'Books have been taken from the reading rooms or defaced. And there was that distressing business with the Portland vase. Many of our exhibits are too large or heavy to make away with. I doubt that anyone could easily remove the whales from the natural history collection although many of the keepers of antiquities rather wish that someone would. But every exhibit has been carefully catalogued and described so that even if smaller items were stolen and someone attempted to sell them, I would hope that any dealer would recognise them. The only danger is, I think, to the gold. There is a room dedicated to gold and silver jewellery, some of it inlaid with precious stones and pearls. But the number of attendants has been increased of late. We engaged more men in January for the exhibition of the priceless Castellani collection. It was featured in the newspapers, so I fear that even those who have never visited the museum would know about it.'

'And these valuable items are constantly watched?' asked Holmes.

'Oh yes, very closely. I ought to mention that this is a critical time for us financially. In the next few months Parliament will be deciding on its annual grant of funds. We are hoping to receive a substantial sum to enable us to enlarge our galleries. Extensive as our displays are there are so many antiquities that we are unable to show simply for lack of space. They are stored in the basement and we cannot allow the public in there because it is dreadfully crowded and too dark to see anything not to mention the stairs, which would be inadvisable for ladies. We need more room.'

Holmes was thoughtful. He leaned forward, intently, chin in his hand. 'Do you think it possible, Dr Martinson, that the incident you have described to me is in any way connected to your current work?'

Martinson looked quite startled by this question. 'Why no — except that my work could be delayed or impeded by it if enquiries proved to be necessary.'

Holmes seemed to absorb this information, then leaned back almost languidly, lightly resting his hands against each other by the fingertips. 'Please describe to me what you are presently engaged upon.'

'Oh — yes, gladly. I have a paper to show you, if you would like to take a look.' Martinson went to his desk, put on his reading spectacles and unrolled the paper scroll.

Holmes in a sudden burst of energy, was swiftly by his side, with a keen expression.

'As you see, Mr Holmes, this is a copy of some hieroglyphs, the ancient form of Egyptian writing. They were carved on the wall of a burial chamber which was recently discovered in Saqqara. There is a mystery concerning this chamber. It lay beneath what had long been supposed to be simply abandoned building rubble. On closer examination this was recognised as the lower level of a small step pyramid, quite broken down; in fact, it is now believed, destroyed not by the actions of time, but deliberately. The burial chamber was empty, and there was no sign that it had ever been used. It was probably only partly completed and abandoned. The hieroglyphs appear on the upper section of one wall. The others are blank. But as you can see here —' he pointed to some of the images — 'the carvings have in places been chipped away. I have established the fact that the sections which have been attacked — there is really no other word for it — were the name of the person whose tomb it was intended to be. The name is enclosed in a shape known as a cartouche which shows that it is that of royalty, and the location and nature of the tomb suggests a pharaoh, but who he might have been we do not know.'

'What of the remainder of the carvings?' asked Holmes. 'Have these been translated? As it is a tomb, I assume they must be a tribute, an account of the man and his deeds?'

'Ah, no it is not. But the words have been translated. They form an incantation to ensure that the deceased will rise from the dead, become an immortal and take his place with the gods. I suppose you might call it a spell. It was believed that reading it or speaking it aloud is all that is needed to animate the dead. The cartouche also has magical properties. It protects the individual named within against evil spirits.'

'But without the name of the deceased —' Holmes concluded.

'Precisely,' said Martinson, nodding energetically. 'The spell will not work, and the pharaoh cannot live again. There are legends of course, passed down by word of mouth. A pharaoh who was so wicked that his own courtiers and family conspired to murder him. Construction of his tomb, always a lengthy process, would have begun during his lifetime, so that on his death it would be ready to ensure his existence in the afterlife. But not only did his enemies kill him, they destroyed his body, and his name, to ensure that he would be erased from existence forever. His name was never to be written or carved or even spoken on pain of death. Nowhere have we discovered any record which tells us his name. He has quite vanished.'

'And you hope to solve the mystery?' asked Holmes, his eyes lighting up with a curious gleam.

'Yes, I do. And I may have the means of doing so. Not long ago the museum acquired a fragment, a piece broken from the wall of the burial chamber and which I think may offer a clue. A recent excavation has discovered other pieces. Next month I will be receiving a delegation of eminent visitors to the museum who will bring what they have, and together, we will study the carvings and hope to make some progress.'

'That is extremely interesting,' said Holmes, 'and now, I would very much like to examine the place where you saw the unusual events.'

'Of course,' said Martinson, 'come this way.'

'And if I might borrow this useful implement?' asked Holmes, picking up the magnifying lens.

'Yes, by all means. I usually walk through the connecting corridor, but as you are new visitors, I would not deny you the pleasure of entry by the front portico,' said Martinson with a smile.

And so, at last I warmed to the thrill of those noble columns. We passed into the entrance hall where a magnificent staircase rose up before us, and traversed a room dominated by the most formidable sculptures of winged bearded men which I was told were Assyrian. Unobtrusive but impressive in a different way were the museum's attendants in their quiet dark uniforms and peaked caps, standing ready to assist visitors and deal with any eventualities.

The long wide Egyptian gallery on the ground floor is an imposing space running almost the length of the great Museum and holds the largest and heaviest of its exhibits.

Martinson was an enthusiastic guide, and I saw Luckhurst, who allowed his uncle to expound uninterrupted on his great passion, smile with affectionate pride. We were assured that this was the most popular location with visitors, and there were many there, both ladies and gentlemen. They moved about almost reverentially, their feet making soft echoing clicks on the stone floor, voices so hushed in comment that the sweep of silken skirts was scarcely as quiet.

The most famous possession about which the public likes to stroll and gather in admiration, is, so Martinson told us, the Rosetta Stone, a massive black slab carved with a decree in three alphabets. It sits on a granite plinth held in a cradle formed of iron bars, which holds it tilted so that its surface which is protected by a framed sheet of glass, can be studied by scholars. Its discovery had enabled the translation of the mysterious hieroglyphs which was achieved by a Frenchman called Champollion.

There were other wonders to see: we were shown the outer casing stones of the greatest of the pyramids, a portion of the beard of the giant sphinx, enormous slabs of limestone that had once formed part of tombs and massive granite sarcophagi. Some statues and even parts of statues were truly colossal; there were giant disembodied heads and arms and feet which made me wonder aloud how large the completed work must have been.

Other smaller statues in stone or even wood were more lifelike, showing men or gods holding spears and about to step forward as if emerging from history into the present. These demonstrated that the Egyptians were perfectly capable of rendering the human form correctly so why they could not or would not do so in flat carvings I shall never understand.

There were sculptures which informed me that the pharaoh Rameses II whom I had seen depicted as a boy on Dr Martinson's illustration, once grown to adulthood liked nothing better than waving a large battle axe and crushing his enemies under his chariot wheels. In subsequent years I have met a number of men who had enjoyed unearned privilege in their early lives and they often made me think of young Rameses II. I do hope he mellowed with age.

Holmes made no comments during our tour, but his eyes moved constantly about the scene, and I sensed that he was absorbing every detail of his surroundings and our guide's descriptions and committing them to memory. Towards the upper end of the gallery, more crowded with a host of lesser exhibits, Dr Martinson paused and said, 'This was the spot.'

Holmes stopped and gave everything a more intense study. 'The light in this location is of course far brighter than it would have been when you saw the events last week. It is hard to assess the truth of the matter without examining the gallery at dusk and after the public have left and preferably with the moon at the same phase, but I assume that that would not be permitted,' he said.

'I am sorry,' said Martinson, 'but it is beyond my authority to allow it.'

Holmes strode up and down, chin on his chest. I could see he was frustrated by this restriction. He suddenly whirled around to face Martinson. 'Show me exactly where you were standing and point out where this procession came from.'

Martinson showed us that he had been standing beside a black granite obelisk when he had first heard the faint sound that announced the approach of the apparitions and had quickly moved behind it to see them emerging from the shadows. 'They came, I believe from the northern end of the gallery, moving directly south. I didn't see where they went. Perhaps they just — I don't know — vanished.'

'I am not convinced of that,' said Holmes. 'They will have left some sort of trace. Everything does if one can see it, but we may have come too late.' He took the magnifying lens from his pocket and began an earnest examination of all the glass and polished wooden surfaces in the area, finally dropping to his knees and giving the same careful attention to the floor, much to the surprise and amusement of some of the visitors, whom he ignored.

At last, he sprang to his feet. 'One question — when you saw the floating light, did you detect any particular odour which might have suggested its origin? Any impression of burning oil, or paraffin, or wax?'

Martinson looked uneasy. 'No, nothing. I am afraid my sense of smell is somewhat deficient. What do you think, Mr Holmes? Can you come to any conclusion?'

Holmes returned the lens to its owner with a touch of regret. 'You must allow me a little time to give the matter some thought,' he said. 'In the meantime, should you ever require my assistance, do not hesitate to call on me. Here is my card. I am to be found at my rooms in Montague Street not far from here, and if not there, I am usually at Barts.'

Our visit was at an end. I was sorry not to have the opportunity to examine the Greek marbles but determined to do so another day. George Luckhurst thanked us, grateful I think, more for the fact that we had come at all, than any prospect of our throwing light on the mystery. He elected to remain with his uncle, and so Holmes and I departed.

'Well,' said Holmes shortly afterwards, as we sat drinking hot coffee at a nearby café. 'What do you make of Dr Martinson's curious experience?'

'I am no expert, but I could see no obvious sign of any disturbance of the mind,' I said. 'Scholarly gentlemen are often a little eccentric in their ways but that is not the same thing as derangement. And I saw no evidence of significant failure of the eyesight. It is not unusual for a gentleman who studies a great deal to require reading glasses. The magnifying glass was not I think suggestive of poor vision, but merely the requirements of his work.'

'Quite,' said Holmes. 'You observed, of course his unusual aversion to fire?'

'He seemed a little worried by it, but I assumed it was because the museum's policy was not to allow it.'

'The museum itself does not employ lighting other than daylight, although it is clearly permitted in the private residences which are in separate wings. His room was fitted for gas, which was not lit, but there were no matches, and I saw no evidence of lamps or candles as a scholar might use to throw additional light on documents. There was a noticeable disturbance in his manner when fire was mentioned, and I also observed a stiffness in the movement of his fingers. I took care when he was pointing out some details of the drawings to observe him closely and there were some unusual creases in the skin of his wrists. At some point probably many years ago, Dr Martinson suffered burns to his hands which were severe enough to require the protection of gloves, and which left him in fear of fire. The impairment to his sense of smell may have been caused by inhalation of smoke or hot air.'

'Is that important do you think?'

'Perhaps. It does explain his reluctance to approach the mysterious light.'

Something suggested itself to me and I ventured, 'I do have one observation to make regarding Dr Martinson's visions. I am reminded of a phenomenon Professor Platt alluded to in one of his lectures. The Brocken illusion. It is experienced by travellers in certain mountain regions when the light and the clouds are configured in a particular way. Although the observers can see strange and marvellous things, they are not deluded nor is there any fault in their eyesight. It is a perfectly natural consequence of the landscape and weather. Sometimes the eye cannot quite comprehend what it sees and so the mind creates a picture which appears to make the best sense it can devise. Perhaps that is why Dr Martinson saw something which reminded him of an Egyptian ritual.'

Holmes looked thoughtful. 'You are suggesting that Dr Martinson chanced to experience an illusion caused perhaps by the character of the light at that precise moment. It may have been assisted by reflections from the glass cases and shadows cast by the standing sculptures. And in his mind, he naturally saw figures created from his own very specific interests?'

'That is my theory,' I said, a little shyly as I could see that he was far from convinced. 'Another man, in the same spot at the same time, might have seen something quite different.'

Holmes put down his cup. 'I would not denigrate your theory, which is an excellent one, and may well be true, neither will I offer one of my own until I have more facts. The unusual noise still requires an explanation.' He gave a little grunt of annoyance and bestowed a sharp rap of a clenched fist on the tabletop. 'How I wish I had been consulted earlier! It was abundantly clear that if there had been any marks left by intruders they have long been occluded or destroyed by the passage of a thousand visitors. And the floating light — any lingering scent or a single drop of wax or trace of ash would have elevated it from the realms of fancy into something far more interesting. Well,' he sighed, 'I must wait and see if Dr Martinson consults me again. But if this was the work of thieves with designs on the collections, it may be that his giving the alarm followed by our presence there will have been sufficient warning and they will decide to go elsewhere. So, the museum's gold is safe after all. But I will write to Luckhurst with our deliberations so far and in the meantime, I have one or two enquiries of my own to pursue.'

CHAPTER FOUR

Several days passed during which I saw little of Holmes and heard nothing more from either George Luckhurst or his uncle. I wondered how much progress Holmes was making in his further enquiries regarding the strange visions of Dr Martinson. I did take the opportunity of consulting Professor Platt about the Brocken illusion, but learned that it was principally associated with the great outdoors and configurations of clouds and mist, and he had never heard of such a thing occurring inside a building. I decided not to press my questioning any further, in case the professor thought I was asking on my own account and decided to have a quiet word with my friends.

One morning in early May, I was engaged in my usual studies at Barts when emerging from the students' library I chanced to encounter Dr Martinson. He looked pale and agitated, and was staring about him in a distracted manner, the state of his grooming far from the neatly turned-out gentleman of our first meeting. When he saw me, it was with obvious relief. 'Oh Mr Stamford,' he exclaimed, 'I am so very pleased to see you! Can you tell me where I might find Mr Holmes? I have been to his lodgings, but the landlady says he has not been there all night, and I am not at all familiar with this place.'

'He is not in the library,' I said. 'Let us try the chemistry laboratory. If he is engrossed in a problem, he can sometimes lose all account of the time. I'll show you the way.'

'He is a very strange fellow,' said Martinson, as he accompanied me, 'but I have the feeling that if anyone can throw light on — well, it is so terrible a thing that I cannot

41

bring myself to say it. And time is of the essence.' His hands, which were still wearing the thin leather gloves, were trembling. Now that Holmes had drawn my attention to it, I could see the thread-like scarring, a faded red, that carved its way up his wrists and disappeared under his cuffs.

I reassured Martinson that I would not leave his side until he had found Holmes, and he thanked me profusely.

Fortunately, we found Holmes in the laboratory. He was standing bent over his workbench examining the progress of a reaction that bubbled in a heated retort. In that posture he resembled a giant crow with dark plumage and a prodding beak, his keen eyes watchful and tireless. How long he had been there it was hard to say, but I sometimes felt that to him, work was better sustenance than sleep or food. If Martinson had been concerned about interrupting his studies, it was unnecessary as was obvious from the way Holmes reacted with anticipation on seeing the visitor that he was delighted to see him. He quickly extinguished his Bunsen burner, allowing the experiment to subside into a pool of hot pungent liquid.

'Martinson, what have you to report? I see that you have come out in a great hurry and have slept little and, I suspect, breakfasted less.'

The Egyptologist subsided onto a stool with a little groan. 'Sleep has been impossible, and I have no appetite. The last few hours have been very nearly the worst ones of my life. But before I say any more, I must ask both you and Mr Stamford to agree to the utmost secrecy. The facts may come out in time. I hope they will not but if they do so without a resolution, the result will be damaging beyond belief. The museum has been closed for cleaning this week, as it is every few months, but it is due to reopen to the public very soon. The delegation to debate the Saqqara fragments is already on its way. I am quite desperate to settle the matter as soon as possible.'

We both agreed to his terms at once. Our visitor was clearly in the grip of a powerful emotion and blotted his brow with a handkerchief as he steadied himself to go on.

'I may not have mentioned this, Stamford,' said Holmes, 'but Dr Martinson has kindly conducted me on an extensive tour of the museum, so I have become familiar with every cranny including places where the public are not normally admitted. As a result,' he added in a lighter tone he must have adopted in an attempt to calm the visitor, 'I have developed a strong sympathy with the keepers of antiquities on the subject of preserved whales.'

'It required a little subterfuge on my part,' Martinson admitted with a shaky smile, 'since I introduced Holmes as a visiting scholar desirous of examining the minor Assyrian sculptures in the basement, and the workshops where our displays are created.'

Holmes drew up a stool and sat facing the Egyptologist, saying nothing but gazing at him earnestly. To our surprise Dr Martinson on trying to tell us his news, began to shake violently, and I believe he was on the verge of tears. Holmes moved swiftly and provided our distressed visitor with a beaker of water which he drank gratefully, and we waited for him to recover.

'It happened last night,' he said. 'The cleaners had departed for the day and the attendants were making their final tour of inspection. There are far fewer of them on duty when the building is closed to the public. I should explain that the senior keepers take it in turns to be always available for periods of twenty-four hours and last night it was my turn. I was in the first-floor Egyptian gallery where we display the mummies, when I heard a terrible cry ring out, a shout of "fire!". I could not tell you its origin, or even identify the speaker, but it shook me to my soul. I at once called out to the attendants to seek it out hoping against hope that it might be a false alarm — we have had them before — or that it could be dealt with and no harm done if we were swift. And then the thought came to me. What if, despite all our precautions and vigilance, thieves had got into the building? Supposing one of them had raised a false alarm to send us all rushing to find a fire while they were actually in another part of the building stealing the gold?

'I asked an attendant to go with me to the gold room, where we were able to reassure ourselves that all was secure. The gold room is in the western wing on the first floor. Then one of the other attendants came to us saying that the fire had been found, but it was a trivial thing, just something smouldering in a clay pot, no flames at all, and it had been dealt with. No damage had been done, and there was no immediate need to call out the fire brigade. Of course, I was relieved to hear it, but all the same I could not help but fear that this was the work of intruders who might still be in the building. I left the first man to guard the gold room and summoned the other attendants to come and report to me, and that was when we realised that two of our men were missing, in fact they had not been seen since before the alarm was raised.

'I was told that Finley who is the chief attendant had gone with one of the junior staff, a youth called Collier to look into a possible disturbance in the workshops. We went to look for them and found them there, both injured and lying on the floor. They had been most savagely attacked and then bound and gagged. We released them, but neither was able to give any coherent account of what had happened to them. Finley carries a set of keys and it was apparent that these had been taken.

And we saw how the thieves had escaped, as the rear exit which is reached from the workshop was unlocked. Obviously, the incident had to be reported to the police. I sent an attendant to notify the constable on point in Great Russell Street. We did what we could for our men and summoned a doctor to attend them.

'There is a set of master keys in a safe and I had those brought out so the museum could be properly secured and I set guards at all the entrance doors until the locks could be changed. At the time we felt as sure as we could be that this was an attempted robbery that had been foiled by swift action and that the culprits of whom we found no sign, had most probably left empty handed. The gold and silver exhibits were safe, the display cases untouched.'

Martinson drew a deep ragged breath before he continued. 'I had one last walk about the galleries to reassure myself that all was safe, and that was when I saw what the thieves had actually accomplished. It was beyond my imagination, and even now, I have turned it over and over in my mind a thousand times, and I cannot think how they had managed it, but they had.'

We looked at him intently, neither of us breaking the silence, as he gathered his nerves to tell us more.

'The Rosetta Stone, Mr Holmes.'

'What, damaged?'

'No, stolen. They had stolen the Rosetta Stone.'

CHAPTER FIVE

I do not know to this day which one of us was more astonished. For a moment or two neither of us could speak.

'It is one of the great treasures of the world!' cried Martinson. 'Beyond value! I cannot begin to describe how I felt. Had my eyes deceived me? I wish they had! Was I dreaming? Was I deranged? But I was neither. It was true.'

Another man, I thought, might have feared for himself, seeing in this loss the collapse of his reputation, even his entire career, but not Martinson, who was concerned only with the theft of the precious artefact. He wiped his handkerchief across his eyes. 'I summoned Dr Birch at once, and we notified the police. Their searches were initially hampered by the dark, but they have been questioning everyone concerned with the museum and local residents who might have witnessed something, and they have restarted their examination in daylight. They too are wondering how the stone might have been removed and carried off.'

'Can you suggest a motive for the robbery?' asked Holmes. 'The stone is as you say beyond price and I doubt that it could be sold. Have there been demands from the Egyptian authorities for its return?'

'No, it is ours by treaty, and we have not had any such demands,' said Martinson. 'The motive I am sorry to say is love of money not history. There was an envelope lying on top of the empty plinth. It bore only the words "Dr Birch". He opened it and I could see that he was deeply shocked by the letter within. We were informed that the stone is safe and undamaged, but the thieves are demanding a ransom for its return. £50,000, Mr Holmes. The audacity! They said that if the money is not forthcoming, they will take the stone out to sea and drop it where it will never be found again. They also warned against involving the police, threatening to destroy the stone if we did, but of course it was too late for that.

'Naturally, Dr Birch turned the letter over to the police at once. Given the threat to the stone, they too have been sworn to secrecy and when interviewing the public, they are not revealing the full details of their enquiries. I cannot begin to imagine what would happen if the newspapers were to hear of it. The public furore would end any chance we might have of retrieving the stone safely. But we are left in a terrible position. And then I thought to consult you. I told Dr Birch of your earlier enquiries and while he was somewhat surprised, he granted his permission provided that you too agree to maintain the utmost secrecy.'

'We must go at once,' said Holmes, springing to his feet, 'there is no time to be lost.'

I was neither invited nor told to remain where I was, but when I followed Holmes and Martinson, they did not object. Holmes did not regard me as an intellectual equal, but I think he appreciated a second point of view from the average reasonable man, the kind who, as the saying goes, was likely to be found on the Clapham omnibus.

Our journey that morning was a strange one. The rattling of the cab which had seemed so sprightly only a few days ago now had an ominous sound. Holmes began by asking Martinson for further details of the ransom letter, but he only knew what he had been told by Dr Birch as he had not seen the contents for himself. All he could tell us was that it was on a single folded sheet of plain notepaper. The envelope as far as he could tell was unremarkable. The name 'Dr Birch' had been written in ink, but in large capital letters, which had been copied over several times.

'An old ploy to disguise the handwriting,' said Holmes. He spent the rest of the journey sunk in thought and I did all I could to provide some words of comfort to Dr Martinson, who now that he had unburdened himself, was on the verge of sinking into a faint of exhaustion and despair.

Our four-wheeler was directed not to Great Russell Street, where, because the museum was closed to the public, the main and side gates were locked, but to the far smaller and less stately rear entrance in Montague Place, which gave access to the reading room and workshops. A constable was guarding the door, and after a word with Martinson we were allowed to enter.

The museum was strangely quiet without its crowds of visitors. There were few footsteps and only the faint echoes of voices. We soon found ourselves at the northern end of the long Egyptian ground floor gallery where some sombre looking attendants were on duty and police constables were employed in searches. The scene was supervised by a venerable looking gentleman with a large bald pate and abundant grey whiskers. To my youthful eyes he appeared to be very ancient, although I now realise that at the time, Dr Samuel Birch was only sixty-two, younger than my present age. How the passage of time can enlighten us!

Martinson introduced us, and I saw Birch's bright intelligent eyes take particular note of Holmes. 'As you may imagine,' he said, 'I have many connections with the universities, and I have heard your name mentioned.'

Holmes did not ask how he had been mentioned and Dr Birch did not elaborate.

Birch glanced at Martinson who was looking a little ashen about the face and was in danger of collapse. He quickly summoned an attendant and ordered that Martinson be taken to his apartments where his manservant would see that he had rest and refreshment. 'Poor fellow,' he said with a sympathetic shake of the head, as our troubled visitor was led away, 'he feels it more deeply than any of us as he was on duty last night. But I attach no blame to him.'

'I hope you will not object to my examining the locations where the crimes have taken place?' asked Holmes.

'As long as your work does not impede the police you have my permission. I shall clear it with Inspector Caldwell when he returns. But come with me, I will show you where the stone once lay.'

If Holmes would have preferred to examine another place first, he did not protest. I had the impression that he knew he was permitted to be there only as a very great favour. As we walked down the gallery, we saw evidence of the work of the cleaners. Long ladders were propped against the walls beside the tall windows, and scaffolding had been erected in places from long poles and thick planking lashed together by ropes. Holmes gazed up at them thoughtfully although it was impossible to know what was on his mind. My only observation was that it was impossible for a large heavy object to be removed through a window. The ventilation was through small areas and very high up.

'The police have been provided with details of our cleaning staff and they are all to be interviewed,' said Birch, helpfully. Holmes merely nodded.

I have to admit, that having seen the famous Rosetta Stone only a week previously I would not have believed it could be stolen had I not that morning seen for myself the empty granite plinth. The stone, its protective glass covering even the metal cradle, were all gone. Holmes walked about the plinth, and taking a magnifying glass from his pocket, which I guessed was a recent purchase, he studied its surface carefully. He then read the descriptive plaque, took a notebook and pencil from his pocket and made a copy of the details.

'The ransom note was found lying on it,' said Birch. 'The inspector has it now.'

'Dr Martinson told us that the thieves demanded a payment of £50,000. Did it say how and when this was to be delivered?'

'Er — no. But I expect that I will receive further instructions in due course.'

'How was the letter written?'

'In capitals, inked over a number of times. I was unable to recognise the hand.'

'You noticed nothing unusual about the paper, or the ink?'

'Nothing at all. The paper and envelope were quite plain, the ink of a very ordinary sort.'

'No marks other than the writing? Smudges? Stains?'

'No, none on the letter. I think the envelope was a little dirty.'

'Any distinctive odour about it?'

'I didn't think to smell it.'

'Was the paper watermarked?'

'I'm afraid I didn't look, but I am sure the police will make enquiries.'

Holmes looked extremely dissatisfied with these replies.

'But as you can see,' Birch went on, 'the great question is how the stone was taken away. It is not an easy thing to transport.'

'Perhaps,' said Holmes, 'in order for me to better consider how the stone might have been removed, I should ask how it was transported here? When did it first arrive?'

'That I can tell you,' said Birch, appearing a little more comfortable with the questioning. 'The stone was brought to England in 1801. At that time the museum exhibits were displayed in a mansion on this very site named Montague House. This was later demolished and replaced by the current building which has been specifically designed for the purpose.'

'How might an object of similar weight and dimensions arrive were it to do so today?'

'Exhibits of that size are transported either in packing crates or in protective wrappings and on arrival at the docks they are lifted by crane onto the back of a carrier wagon which is equipped with a windlass. The wagon enters the museum forecourt by the side gates where our attendants bring a suitable stout trolley or barrow, and the exhibit is hoisted onto it. We have specially constructed barrows with reinforced wheels and beds. It is then brought through a service entrance to the workshop for the packing to be dismantled and any cleaning to be done before it is put on display.'

'The weight of the stone is 1,680lb,' said Holmes, reading from his notes.

'Even with the metal cradle and the glass case it would have weighed less than a ton,' said Birch.

'So, a stone of that size and weight would have been wheeled into the gallery on a barrow. How would it have been lifted onto the plinth?'

'There is a portable hoist which is kept in the workshop. This would have been brought to the spot and assembled and the stone lifted from the barrow onto the plinth. We have handled far larger and heavier exhibits as you can see.'

'The stone is not bolted to the cradle?'

'No, it fits exactly into it, as it was custom made, neither is the cradle attached to the plinth. It lies there by its own weight. It cannot be removed without very considerable effort.'

Holmes was silent for a few moments and I guessed that he was considering the probable chain of events. 'I am sure this will be hard to estimate, but from the time the cleaners left the gallery to Dr Martinson discovering the robbery how much time had elapsed?'

'In May the cleaners leave the building shortly before five o'clock. I expect the constable on point will have a note of when he was alerted, but I can't imagine given what has been described to me both by Martinson and the attendants, that it can have been more than twenty minutes.'

Once again Holmes fell silent in thought.

'How do you think it can have left the building?' I asked.

'That is an interesting question since the thieves must have chosen their time very carefully,' said Birch. 'Perhaps they knew that there would be fewer attendants on duty this week. But they might not have anticipated the difficulties they would face. Because they acted during our closure for cleaning, they could not have removed the stone from the front of the museum. Even if they had managed to bring it out of the service entrance, they would have found all the front gates securely locked, chained and padlocked. The keys are held in a safe and this has not been forced. I am quite sure they did not leave that way. Also, Great Russell Street is a busy thoroughfare, with shops and restaurants, where there is always a policeman on point. The removal of a large item being winched onto a vehicle would have been seen, and police enquiries have not come up with any witnesses to unusual movements.'

'We came in today from the Montague Place entrance,' I said. 'Do you think it could have been taken out there?'

'That is the only explanation I can think of,' said Birch. 'It is the only exit possible if we exclude Great Russell Street. There are the entrances to the keepers' apartments, but they are all approached by stairs and in any case are far too narrow to permit any kind of barrow to pass. And an exhibit of that weight would have had to be transported by barrow.'

'There are larger items in the museum which are housed on the first floor,' said Holmes, who had been listening very carefully to our conversation. 'I assume they cannot have been brought up by the main stairs?'

'No,' said Birch, 'but the side staircases have specially designed vertical stairwells to enable large items to be raised by hoist.'

'That would be a lengthy procedure.'

'Oh yes, it has to be done with great care and can take several hours to achieve. I can assure you that the stone is nowhere on the upper floor.'

'The basement has no such stairwell.'

'Indeed, that is a part of the original building, and is not designed for the transport of large or heavy items. Any exhibits to be stored there must be suitable to be taken down by manpower only. Barrows and hoists cannot be used.'

'It is quite a mystery,' I said.

'Oh no!' said Holmes, with a sudden gleam lighting up his eyes, 'it is not *one*, but *several* mysteries all wrapped up together. And now, Dr Birch, I would be very obliged if you would show me where this fire was discovered.'

CHAPTER SIX

We ascended the great central staircase and on reaching the upper floor followed Dr Birch as he turned right to the eastern galleries. These, as well as the north-east and south-eastern rooms were devoted entirely to the museum's natural history collection. Even if I had not known that there had been a fire it was by now apparent, since there was a very pronounced odour of burning which grew stronger the closer we approached the saloons in the far corner of the building.

'Of course, I am very sympathetic to the requirements of Professor Owen whose splendid collection this is,' said Dr Birch, 'however I feel it will be a big improvement when the natural history exhibits have their own museum. Unfortunately, that is not due to be completed for several years.'

I could not help wondering how the numerous examples of flora and fauna had been preserved and what was the potential risk in case of fire from the release of vapour from poisonous chemicals. Some of the mammals were merely skeletons but others, even quite substantial ones such as the great cats, were a fine tribute to the art of the taxidermist and were displayed in a life-like manner. Most of the specimens were enclosed in wall cases but the larger items, rhinoceros and giraffes, were free standing on plinths. The much-disparaged whales, which were of immense size, were suspended above the cases of dolphins. At the north-eastern corner of the museum was a saloon devoted to fossils and molluscs, with glass cases hung on every wall labelled with descriptions of the items displayed.

In the centre of the floor stood a rough clay pot about eighteen inches high, part filled with sand from which some blackened material protruded. Beside it was an empty fire bucket.

'There were no flames, only smoke,' said Birch.

'Was it easily extinguished?' asked Holmes, peering into the pot.

'Not as easily as might be supposed,' said Birch. 'Our attendants are all instructed what to do in case of fire. One of them brought the fire bucket and threw sand into the pot, then when that appeared to have no effect, he used the bucket to cover the pot, imagining that this would stop the smouldering by cutting off the air, but despite this it continued to smoke. He then went to fetch water, but by the time he had returned, whatever the material was had all burnt to ash. The pot appears to be a very ordinary one such as might be purchased in any market,' Dr Birch continued. 'Inspector Caldwell does not think anything can be learned from it.'

'And yet,' said Holmes, 'a great deal may be learned from this humble item. Has it been moved, or is this where it was found last night?'

'I believe it was found just here.'

Holmes looked about him as if measuring with his eyes the distance from the pot to the walls of the saloon. He then knelt on the floor beside the pot and crawled around it, examining its surface with his magnifying glass. Finally, he tilted the pot carefully and examined the base, when he gave a little exclamation of satisfaction.

'What have you found?' I asked.

'A small smear as if made with a fingertip. Dark red, probably blood. Too little to subject to a chemical test. The inspector may make of that what he can.' Holmes sniffed at the contents of the pot, his nostrils flaring as he inhaled the odour. 'Interesting,' he said. 'I think this material warrants more detailed examination.' Using his penknife, he carefully moved aside the sand to uncover some of the burnt matter, lifted out a sample and placed it in an envelope he took from his pocket. 'The inspector need not be concerned that I am removing evidence, I have left more than enough for him to examine.' Holmes stood up sealing the envelope and replacing it in his pocket. 'The material was lit with a match which is now no more than a blackened twig and I fear there is nothing to be learned from it. And now, I wish to see the workroom where the attack on the men took place. Are they recovered enough to be questioned?'

'The inspector has sent his sergeant round to speak to them,' said Birch. 'I heard from the doctor last night that Finley was too unwell to give any account of what occurred. The injury has been dressed and a nurse engaged to care for him. Collier has a lump on the head which he declares is too painful to be touched, but he is rather better, and needs only a night's rest. We may learn more from him.'

'Who discovered them?'

'One of the other attendants, Robson. Collier lodges with his family.'

'I would like to speak to him.'

'I'll have him brought to you.'

We descended to the ground floor by a side staircase and Birch led us to a large workshop, which was laid out with benches where artefacts such as painted pottery and figurines were being cleaned or restored.

There was a strong chemical odour which reminded me somewhat of the dissecting room at Barts although without the additional pronounced stench of putrefaction. Deep shelves were stocked with jars of liquid chemicals and powders, and there were numerous racks and trays of instruments. On one table a display was under construction of gracefully arranged branches on which perched exotic looking birds with colourful plumage and long curved beaks. A label declared them to be African sunbirds, and I stopped to admire them and could not help but imagine them alive and gorgeous in the tropical heat.

There was a stock of packing materials and small crates piled in one corner, and some of the poles and planks of scaffolding were leaning against a wall beside the substantial metal struts, wheels and chains of a hoist. There were also a number of barrows for the transport of exhibits. The smaller ones were suitable only for relatively lightweight items, but two rather larger ones had long heavy flat bases and thick wheels.

The scene of the attack was quite obvious as there were smears and spots of blood on the floor.

Holmes said nothing but surveyed the room with great care, paying particular attention to the marks on the floor, although he also studied the scaffolding materials and the hoist in some detail. Birch watched him and I could see that he was impressed by the meticulous manner in which my friend studied his surroundings. Birch had sent a man to fetch the attendant Robson and Holmes paused in his work as soon as he arrived. He was a strong looking man of about thirty, but from his manner still very shaken by the events of the previous night.

'Robson,' said Birch, 'this is Mr Holmes, who is advising us, and his assistant Mr Stamford. Please answer any questions they might have.'

As Holmes' assistant I did my best to look assured and intelligent. Holmes did rather better than I managed in those departments. Although we were the same age, his towering height and air of confidence gave him a mature authority beyond his years, whereas I was rather boyish in appearance and remained so well into my thirties.

'I understand, Robson, that you found Finley and Collier in this room last night?' asked Holmes.

'I did, sir.'

'Where, and in what condition?'

'They were both lying on the floor here, sir, face down.' He pointed to the area of blood smears. 'Finley was just there where the blood is. I'm not sure Collier bled much, if at all.'

'Side by side?'

'About two or three feet apart, I would say. When I walked in, I could hear groaning. It was hard to see exactly what the matter was, as it was almost dark, but I gathered that both had been injured. They had been tied up with ropes, hand and foot, and rags stuffed into their mouths, so I untied them and tried to bring them round.'

'Do you have the ropes and gags?'

'I think the police took them away, sir. They looked for a weapon, but they didn't find one.'

'Was either of the men able to say what had happened to them? Try your best to remember exactly, as first impressions can be the most valuable.'

'Well, sir, Finley, he was trying to talk but it came out quite peculiar, and I couldn't make out what he was saying. Collier, once he came to himself, was a bit brighter. He said Finley thought he had heard a suspicious noise in the workshop and asked him to accompany him to see what the matter was. They were looking about them when he heard someone come up behind him. Before he had a chance to warn Finley, he felt a blow on his head and knew nothing more until he found himself lying on the floor with me untying his hands. I called Dr Martinson and he saw to it that they were looked after.'

'One more thing, may I inspect your boots?'

Robson looked surprised but complied.

Holmes studied the shape and markings on the soles, then he made a little sketch in his notebook.

'Collier lodges with you I believe?' asked Birch.

'He does sir.'

'How is he today?'

'Well enough sir, though he didn't have the most restful night, what with the wife having had twins last month. Didn't do his headache no good at all.'

Birch thanked Robson who returned to his duties. 'Well, Mr Holmes, what do you think?' asked Birch.

'Former military though not recently,' said Holmes. 'His general bearing and habit of neatness even under difficult circumstances attest to that. And a little deaf in one ear.'

Birch raised his eyebrows. 'That is so. He has been with us some five years and has always proved reliable and truthful. As to what happened last night,' he added, 'Inspector Caldwell has a theory to explain how the thieves got in. It's too much to suppose that a large gang of men managed to slip into the museum past the cleaners without being noticed. But one man might. Caldwell believes that one of the thieves entered the museum by the Montague Place entrance and hid in the workshop. Any men working there would have gone home by then. There is enough space behind the scaffolding planks to conceal a man. The thief waited there, and then when the two attendants arrived, he knocked them out, tied them up, stole the keys and let in his confederates. One of them set the smoke material smouldering and gave the alarm. The other thieves waited their time. Once the other attendants had gone to deal with the fire, the thieves came out of hiding and did their work.'

'There are several obvious flaws in that theory,' said Holmes, 'but I will comment further when I have more facts. I am sorry to say that multiple feet have disturbed the bloodstains on the floor. There are traces of police issue boots which are very distinctive, and also those worn by the attendants. But there are other marks here which are far less distinct. Soft slippers perhaps with felt soles such as are worn by burglars, which make almost no noise and leave no distinct print. What type of boots do the cleaners wear? Stout workmen's boots I should imagine?'

'I believe so, yes.'

'These soft soles have carried the smears around the main area of staining, but the amount of blood is so slight that they do not go very far, and it is impossible to follow them and show where they lead. But I think I can identify different sizes. As expected, we are looking at several intruders.'

Holmes now turned his attention to the two large barrows. One was rather more substantial than the other, and each had a polished metal plaque attached, stamped with the maximum weight they could safely transport. Holmes wrote the details in his notebook, and then taking a measuring tape from one of the benches, measured both barrows and noted the results. 'Are these always kept here?' he asked.

'I believe they are, but I would need to confirm that with the workshop manager,' said Birch. 'There are other smaller barrows in the reading room for the movement of books, but these are the ones principally employed to transport exhibits.'

'What of the monumental sculptures? Many of them must weigh several tons, far beyond what these barrows can transport. How are they moved?'

'Extreme transport measures are needed but because they are only required on rare occasions, they are hired in. We have none in the museum.'

Holmes pulled at the steering handle of the smaller of the two stouter barrows, which moved with relative ease. The larger one, however, presented more difficulty and after a moment or two of effort, he took out his magnifying glass, bent down, and studied the wheels and their connection to the axles.

He was about to question Birch further when the door opened, and a man walked in bearing himself like one used to command. Above middling height, and very broad in build, he was about fifty years of age, his sparse greying hair more than compensated for by a dark luxuriant beard and moustache, and thick brows. He favoured Holmes and me with deeply suspicious looks.

'Ah, Inspector,' said Birch. 'Mr Holmes and Mr Stamford are assisting the museum in these difficult and delicate circumstances. Gentlemen, this is Detective Inspector Caldwell of Scotland Yard.'

Anyone who has read Dr Watson's reminiscences will be aware of Holmes' frequently expressed contempt for the police, and how few individual policemen he actually tolerated in company. This was partly due, I believe, to the fact that many policemen were understandably unhappy about the involvement of unqualified amateurs into what they saw as their professional preserve. At the same time, since Holmes was superior in intellect to most men, he could not therefore fail to be above the mental capacity of the average police officer. This undoubtedly led to some friction, which was only mollified by Holmes being more than content to allow the police to take all the credit for the cases which he solved. If the birth of the antagonism can be laid at the door of one man, however, that man is undoubtedly Detective Inspector Caldwell of Scotland Yard.

CHAPTER SEVEN

'You may dismiss your young assistants,' snapped the inspector, without affording us a second glance. 'I will report only to you, Dr Birch.'

Dr Birch smiled, appeasingly. 'It would be more convenient for me if they were to remain. They know all that has occurred. I keep no secrets from them.'

Caldwell gave a snort of annoyance. 'Very well, if you insist, but they must not interfere in police business.'

I did my best to appear inoffensive. Holmes said nothing but there was a dangerous glitter in his eyes.

'You will be relieved to know that we have made considerable progress in finding your stone,' announced the inspector, 'and I am confident that it will be back in your hands by tomorrow.' Holmes raised an eyebrow at this ambitious statement. 'There is a definite trail, and my men are following it. You will recall that the ransom note threatened to drop the stone into the sea. Unwittingly the thieves provided us with a valuable clue. We believe it has been taken to the docks and is being held aboard a ship.'

'Do you know how it was conveyed there?' asked Dr Birch.

'Yes, we do; in fact, we now know the whole of their cunning scheme. They are clever thieves, or their scheme would not have succeeded, but they will never be able to outwit a detective inspector of thirty years' experience. I have seen almost everything in my time, Dr Birch, and apart from the unique nature of the artefact, I have investigated many thefts of this nature before. Only one thing surprises me, that the little note they left supplied no details of where to deliver the ransom money, or even a suggestion that further instructions will follow. That is very unusual.'

'Is it?' said Birch. 'I must take your word for it, I suppose.'

'It is. But I feel sure that you will receive another note very soon, and it should be passed to me without delay.'

'I am still quite mystified by the whole event, of course,' said Dr Birch. 'But I am reassured by your confidence. Could you enlighten me as to how they managed it?'

Caldwell gave a superior smile. 'As we discussed earlier today, their first action was for one intruder to slip into the museum unnoticed, where he lay in wait for Mr Finley, and stole the keys in order to admit his confederates, who must have been lurking in the dark nearby. They had already arranged for a suitable vehicle to be hired and it was waiting outside for them. As you know, Montague Place is a quiet residential street. There were few passers-by, and since it was generally advertised that the museum was closed for cleaning any activity by men appearing to be at work would not have excited suspicion.' The inspector dug into a capacious pocket, drew out a well-worn notebook and thumbed through the pages. 'My constables have been interviewing local residents and we have five witnesses — two gentlemen, two ladies and a boy. They have confirmed that a wagon of the sort used to deliver heavy goods, drawn by two horses and fitted with a windlass was seen in Montague Place last night. Not long afterwards, some men were seen leaving the museum. They were pushing a barrow which appeared to bear a large amount of rolled up carpet. This was brought aboard the wagon by windlass and the vehicle was then driven away. One of the witnesses said that he simply assumed that some carpets were being taken to be cleaned.'

'That is understandable,' said Dr Birch. 'But it still astonishes me that they were able to remove the stone from its plinth and transfer it in such a short time. Had our men done so it would have taken rather longer.'

Caldwell was undeterred by this objection. 'That suggests to me that they had considerable expertise in such things. Our next step therefore is to conduct interviews with businesses which specialise in removals of that nature. I think the thieves must have taken the hoist from your workroom, erected it over the plinth and then lifted the stone onto one of your barrows. They then wheeled it to the exit where the vehicle was waiting. If they were smart enough it would not have taken them long.'

I glanced at Holmes who looked about to make a comment but then thought better of it and clamped his mouth closed in a severe line.

'Have you learned anything more from Finley and Collier?' asked Birch. 'I am extremely anxious about them, especially Finley who was in a very bad way last night. Are they fit to be interviewed?'

'I have sent my sergeant to question them. I will let you know once he has reported,' said Caldwell. With a respectful nod to Dr Birch, he bustled briskly away.

Birch turned to Holmes. 'Well, we do know more now.'

'Do we?' said Holmes cynically.

Birch glanced at his pocket watch. 'It is about time I took a bite of luncheon. If you would join me, we can talk further.'

We agreed and were conducted to Dr Birch's apartments, which were far less austere than those of Dr Martinson and displayed the warmth and comfort of a family home that only domestic happiness and affection can provide. Mrs Birch and her daughters made us very welcome and regaled us with the best luncheon any young student could have wished for. We were told that Dr Martinson had been given a light breakfast and was even now sleeping the sleep of exhaustion. There was no mention of the theft at the family table, but once we had enjoyed our luncheon, we repaired to Dr Birch's study where, surrounded by shelves of handsomely bound volumes and displays of Oriental art, we made ourselves comfortable and the discussion continued.

'The inspector is undoubtedly a man of experience,' said Birch. 'What do you make of him?'

'Apart from the fact that he is a widower, was a pugilist in his youth and has an old injury to his left elbow, very little,' said Holmes. He was amused by our stares. 'The carriage of the arm and slight thickening of the ears were clear indications. As was the wedding ring on his watch chain.'

'Ah,' said Birch. 'Now you mention it, yes. But I can see that you were not entirely convinced by his theory. It does not seem entirely unreasonable to me.'

'But the whole scheme as he sees it seems to rely on a certain amount of luck,' said Holmes. 'There are any number of points at which it could have failed, but it did not. There is the confederate who managed to slip into the building unnoticed. Then the swiftness with which he was able to acquire the keys. Then there are the barrows, one of which I can see is the right size to transport the stone, conveniently waiting to be used. Let us remind ourselves that these men succeeded in taking a large heavy stone with such smooth efficiency that the plinth is not even scratched and remove it entirely from the building. Had they had hours to do so, I would be less surprised. But it was all done in minutes.'

'Now that you put it that way,' Birch observed, 'it does seem like a tall order.'

'Even so it was not entirely smooth. Every plan has its unexpected obstacles. I noted from my examination of the larger barrow that it had a crack in the wheel assembly, no doubt from the large weight it was being asked to carry. The wheel no longer runs true. Its maximum load is 15 hundredweight, and the stone with its cradle and glass case will weigh somewhat more. But it served the purpose, and once unburdened they were able to return it without difficulty.'

'Do you have a theory, Mr Holmes?'

'Let us look at the facts and see where they lead us,' said Holmes. 'We will start with the setting of the pot of smoke. It is clear to us all that this was a very carefully planned distraction. Nothing was left to chance. First of all, the contents of the pot, whatever they were, and that I hope to determine, were specifically designed to create only a great deal of smoke and no flame. By containing the fire in a clay pot there was little danger of it spreading. Also, please note the location where it was found — the fossils and mollusc saloon, where there is nothing readily flammable, and therefore no danger of a serious fire. The plan was to create a diversion, to draw the attendants to the spot, and provide them with something that they could deal with without needing to summon the fire brigade, which would have impeded the activities of the thieves. The saloon is also located far from the scene of the actual intended crime.'

'Hmm,' said Birch, 'I see your point. Even if the removal of the stone from the ground floor gallery had made some noise, it would not have been heard in all the commotion on the first floor. By the time the smoke had been dealt with and the police advised, the thieves had gone.' He looked thoughtful. 'It is an interesting coincidence that they chose the very night when Martinson was the man on duty. Or was it a coincidence?

I am beginning to wonder. I expect young George Luckhurst has told you how nervous his uncle is of fire?' Birch shook his head. 'Dreadful tragedy.'

'It is a painful subject on which my friend is notably reticent,' said Holmes, evenly. 'I fear he has not apprised me of all the details.'

'That is quite understandable,' said Birch. 'Well, you may not know it, but Martinson has a heroic streak. He and Luckhurst's mother were brother and sister and very devoted. He was at the Luckhurst home one night when a fire broke out. It is thought that a lively puppy dog, Mrs Luckhurst's favourite pet, was frisking as they do, and upset a lantern. Martinson made desperate attempts to save the Luckhursts, rushing through the flames and suffering terrible burns. Sadly, both perished. Martinson would have died too, but after being beaten back twice, the firemen were obliged to seize him to stop him running in again. Their servant Greenleaf only lived because he jumped from a window, but in doing so broke his leg. The injury still troubles him. Fortunately, young Luckhurst was at boarding school at the time. Of course, Martinson was distraught, and he has been a changed man ever since. Quieter, more studious. He cannot bear a lantern near him and is nervous even around candles and tapers.'

That certainly explained why Martinson had been so agitated at the unusual light in his strange vision. I glanced at Holmes and wondered if he was thinking the same, but he was moving on to his next point.

'The next question,' Holmes said, 'is how the stone was lifted so cleanly. Inspector Caldwell has made up his mind that the thieves used the museum's own hoist which they took from the workshop. But he has clearly not examined it as closely as I did. Perhaps not at all. The hoist has been oiled but it was not done recently. I estimate that it has not been used for some weeks. There is a noticeable layer of dust adhering to the oil which is undisturbed. The apparatus was certainly not used last night.'

'You should mention that to the inspector,' said Birch, earnestly.

Holmes gave a sardonic smile. 'Unfortunately, the inspector strikes me as a man who makes up his mind quickly and will not be shaken from his opinion thereafter, no matter what fresh facts emerge. A man must always be prepared to admit that he is wrong.'

'They must have brought their own hoist,' said Birch, 'which was easily done if they hired a vehicle. Perhaps one of the witnesses saw it when the wagon arrived. I will mention it to the inspector.'

'They left little to chance,' said Holmes. 'That is my point. This crime has the hallmark of something that has been meticulously planned, perhaps over several weeks. The expert preparation, location and the timing of the smoke distraction says as much. And they planned it to take place during the museum's closure, when there are fewer attendants, and workmen going in and out would not have looked suspicious. There was even a rehearsal, no doubt to be certain of their route in the near darkness.'

'Rehearsal?' exclaimed Birch.

'I believe so.'

'You can't mean — surely not — that curious vision that Martinson reported?'

'I mean precisely that. We have yet to learn what was done that night, and how many men were involved. The unusual lighting and reflection in the gallery, and Martinson's panic might have amplified the numbers he thought he saw.'

'But nothing was taken,' Birch protested.

'Nothing was supposed to be taken,' replied Holmes.

Birch was thoughtful. 'I recall Finley mentioning that that night he was the last to leave and he found some visitors in the Elgin gallery after closing time, saying that they had got lost, and escorted them out. It's not an uncommon occurrence. I wondered at the time whether all that Martinson saw was some lost visitors trying to find their way out, in fact I said as much to him, but he couldn't agree.'

'They may have been members of the gang making their exit,' said Holmes. 'The police should obtain a description of them once Finley is well enough to be questioned.'

'I will make sure to suggest it to the inspector,' said Birch.

'But you do see what this means,' said Holmes.

Birch looked puzzled. 'I'm not sure that I do.'

'At least one member of the gang has been working in the museum, quite possibly for some while. He was not merely a visitor — he had too much detailed knowledge for that. If it was a fairly recent appointment, then he has been thoroughly acquainting himself with the building and its staff and operations and has been keeping his associates informed. Or it be might someone who has worked here for many years and was offered a bribe.'

'We have more than a hundred employees,' exclaimed Birch, alarmed.

'They must all be questioned.'

I felt sorry for Dr Birch who, only moments before, had been given the hope of a swift resolution by the police only to be faced with the necessity of a long and laborious enquiry by Holmes.

'Tell me as much as you know about the two injured men, Finley and Collier,' said Holmes.

'Well, Harold Finley is about forty-five, he is a good solid man who has been with us for more than twenty years and is reliable and trustworthy. I would stake my reputation on his honesty. He lives not far from the museum with his wife and four children.'

'What of his build — is he a tall man?'

'A little over the average height, I would say, well built, strong and active.'

'And what of Collier?'

'Henry Collier is a recent recruit, aged about twenty or so. He is one of the new men we brought in when we displayed the Castellani gold collection in January. He was previously a porter at the London Regent Hotel which gave him an excellent character. As you know, he lodges with Robson. He has no family in London; they live out Epping way. He has been an exemplary employee, not afraid of hard work. In build he is rather slight, perhaps about your height Mr Stamford, or even a little under.'

'That is interesting,' said Holmes, 'because I would imagine that a thief wishing to disable two men who are standing not too far apart, would choose to strike down the larger man first, as he is the greater threat. Even in the half-dark the difference in size would have been apparent. Yet according to Robson, Collier said that he was struck first.'

'Perhaps it was a failure of memory, confusion after the blow on the head,' I suggested, although as soon as the words were out of my mouth there was something about the issue that began to trouble me.

'Do the police know what type of weapon was used?' asked Holmes.

'They believe it was a cudgel of some kind, perhaps a stout stick weighted with lead. It has not been found. The attacker must have taken it with him.'

'I assume that both men were wearing the peaked caps of their uniforms?'

'Yes, although they are not designed as protection against injury.'

'May I see them? The ones Finley and Collier were wearing?'

'I think the police have them. And the ropes and gags.'

Holmes was disappointed but it was a reply he had been expecting. 'But here are some important points that seem to have escaped the inspector's notice,' he said. 'There are serious flaws lying at the outset of this carefully planned crime. First of all, the requirement for a man to slip past the cleaning staff and into the museum unnoticed. Failure to do so would prevent the entire scheme. Then there is the need for this man to obtain the keys and let in his associates. Finley, as senior attendant, carried the keys. But how did the intruder, lying in wait, know that Finley and not another attendant would enter the workshop?'

'I see what you mean,' said Birch. 'Perhaps the intruder planned to waylay him, and it was just chance that he arrived then?'

'Does it not seem strange that he intended to waylay Finley in the dusk, in a large building when he could have no idea where he might find him?' said Holmes. 'How would he locate the man he wanted without encountering another attendant and being apprehended? What was the chance that Finley would enter the workroom unless he was deliberately lured there?'

'That is true,' Birch admitted.

'Why waste time with such a scheme?' added Holmes. 'They had no time to waste.'

'The thing is...' I said. Holmes looked at me. I admit I quailed a little under that penetrating gaze but soldiered on. 'When I was eight or nine years of age, I was climbing a tree when a branch broke, and I fell and hit my head and was knocked out. The last thing I can remember before the accident is hearing the branch crack and the next thing I knew I was being carried into the house. I don't remember the fall and I don't remember hitting my head. My mother was very anxious about my having no memory of it, but the doctor said that it was perfectly normal in the circumstances, and nothing to worry about. It's one of those things you read in boys' adventure stories, when the hero feels a blow on the head, and it all goes dark. But that's not how it really happens.'

'But Collier said...' Birch stopped.

'Stamford, you have it! That is the last piece of the puzzle!' exclaimed Holmes. 'I had suspected Collier, but now I am certain of it. Let us assume that Collier is one of the gang of thieves, and we cannot therefore trust his account of events. He told Robson that Finley asked him to go to the workshop to investigate a noise, but what if it had been the other way about? Collier, who knew that Finley was the key-holder, reported hearing a noise in the workshop and lured him there. That is how Finley came to be there at just the right moment. There is no need for another confederate to try and slip into the building without being seen, a risky business at best.

'Collier accompanied Finley to the workshop, struck him down, tied him up and took the keys, then he let in the rest of the gang. It might even have been Collier who placed the clay pot which we must assume was already to hand, concealed somewhere, and set it smoking, leaving behind a faint smear of Finley's blood. He gave the alarm, returned to the workshop, where his associates tied him up to avoid suspicion, and when he was found claimed that he had been attacked. I was wondering why the more slightly built man was the less injured of the two. Remember he said that the wound was too painful to be touched? I think an examination would have revealed the truth. He was not injured at all.'

'So Collier was the confederate?' said Birch. 'No wonder he was so active and eager to learn! We had better ensure he doesn't run away.'

'There is no danger of that at present,' said Holmes. 'If he thinks he isn't suspected he will simply return to his work here in due course. Running away now would only draw suspicion.'

'I shall insist that the police take him into custody at once,' said Birch. 'And he should be thoroughly examined by a surgeon. Who knows, once he realises that he is due to be charged with a serious crime he might be persuaded to reveal the names of the rest of the gang, and where they have taken the Rosetta Stone.' Birch rubbed his hands together. 'Your assistance has been invaluable, Holmes. I have no doubt at all that you are right, and if the police act fast we may have the stone back very soon.'

At that moment there was a knock on the door and the maid announced the arrival of Inspector Caldwell and Sergeant Lestrade.

The new arrivals did not have the air of triumph we had hoped for, however. Caldwell's red face was set in a dogged stare, and the sergeant, a beady eyed fellow barely tall enough for a policeman, was grasping his notebook as if it was a holy tract he dared not let fall.

Birch rose to his feet sensing the grim mood they had brought with them. 'What is it? What has happened? Has Finley taken a turn for the worse?'

'He should recover in time,' said Caldwell. 'The man has a thick skull, fortunately for him. No, it's young Collier. I'm afraid he's dead.'

CHAPTER EIGHT

I don't believe I have ever seen Holmes so shocked as he was in that instant, when he saw his carefully described theories suddenly collapse. Only minutes ago, he had been declaring that a man should be prepared to admit that he was wrong. This did not seem to be the best moment to remind him.

'What was the cause of his death?' he demanded.

'Well now, I would say from my long experience that it was the tap on the head he had just received,' said Caldwell, sarcastically, 'but I'm content to leave the fine detail to the inquest.' He glanced at Birch with a sympathetic shake of the head, jerking a thumb at Holmes. 'I wouldn't want this dull spark in the police force.'

Lestrade was unsuccessfully trying to restrain a derisive grin.

'I thought you would want to know as soon as possible as the deceased was employed by you,' Caldwell went on. 'Is there any family that need to be informed?'

'Yes,' said Birch, sadly. 'They live in Epping, I believe.'

'I shall send a telegram to the Epping police and they will see that the family receive a visit, and are told when to attend the inquest,' said Caldwell.

'Poor fellow, so very young,' said Birch. 'It will be a terrible shock to them.'

'All the more reason for us to press on with our enquiries as quickly as possible,' said Caldwell. 'We don't want those brutes on the loose any longer than need be. The sooner we get a rope round their necks the better.' He hurried away with his sergeant in tow.

'Never mind, Mr Holmes,' said Birch soothingly, 'I am sure the truth will come out. And for my part I think you may well be right that there was no intruder who slipped in and one of our attendants was a confederate. It must have been that man who told Finley about the supposed intruder and Collier just went along to assist. It only remains to discover who it was. If the police do not question them all, then I certainly will.' He sighed. 'I will write a letter of condolence to Collier's family and see if there is anything we can do for them.'

Holmes gave Birch his card. 'If you learn any more please let me know at once,' he said, 'I am to be found either at my home or Barts. I will continue to give the matter some thought, but of course I do not expect the police to pay any attention to my observations.'

As we left the museum, Holmes was deep in thought, then after some minutes of silence which I decided not to interrupt, he turned to me. 'Stamford, may I rely on you for some assistance?'

'Yes, of course,' I said.

'Good. I shall be making some enquiries of my own, but you can expect to receive a note. By the way,' he added, 'Dr Birch is a very poor liar.' With that rather disquieting observation, he walked away in the direction of Montague Street.

The next morning I arrived at Barts to be handed a sealed envelope by a fellow student. 'It was that queer chap Holmes who left it for you. Said it was urgent,' he said.

I extracted the note which read simply: *Inquest. 10am. King's Head Tavern Bloomsbury.*

'Not bad news I hope?' asked the student anxiously, and I realised that my face must have revealed my disquiet. I was supposed to be at an important lecture at that hour.

'Please make my excuses,' I said. 'I have to attend an inquest.'

The tavern in question was only a mile away in what was known in those days as Broad Street. The King's Head was commonly used for Bloomsbury inquests, probably more for the size of its accommodation than its comfort or cleanliness. It was a venerable pile dating from the time of the notorious St Giles rookery, a nest of poverty and filth that had once been the haunt of thieves, vagabonds and beggars. Thankfully that maze of squalor had been demolished or I might not have dared venture near it. I'm not sure if the old tavern is there anymore. Broad Street is gone, having been absorbed into the lower end of High Holborn.

I found the upper meeting room of the King's Head attended by the usual interested parties, the coroner's officers, relatives and friends of the deceased and newspaper men who sat absorbed in their notebooks and clutching pencils. I decided to take one of the few unoccupied seats to one side of the gathering. It was usual for a number of cases to be heard at one session, so I was not able to determine if any of Collier's family was there. Inspector Caldwell was a solid presence, and I rather hoped he would not notice me. If he did, he gave no sign of it. I was hoping to see Holmes there, but he was not. I realised then that I had been sent by him as a kind of deputy, to watch on his behalf while he was busy with his own separate pursuits. Some men might have been a little annoyed to have been dispatched on an errand in such a brusque manner, but I must admit I was initially quite flattered by Holmes' trust. On reflection, however, I realised that as the only other person not directly connected with the museum who knew all the facts, I was the only choice. I am not a brave man, unlike Watson who always seemed to think the more dangerous the adventure was the better. Now that the case had been transformed by stages from a fascinating mystery to a theft and then to a murder, I could not help feeling rather nervous and wondering what I had become involved in.

The inquest was presided over by Dr William Hardwicke, the coroner for central Middlesex, who announced that the first case on his list was that of Henry Collier aged twenty-two, who had died at his lodgings in Bury Street the previous night. As he said this, I heard a sob and saw a woman in the row in front of mine turn to the man at her side for comfort. She looked old enough to be the mother of the deceased, and certainly distraught enough. The man I guessed to be Mr Collier was a stout, strong looking fellow. I didn't see his face, for he stared straight ahead, but the hand that patted his wife's shoulder was thick and gnarled, a labourer's hand. I wondered if he worked on the land or perhaps the railways. A much younger man was seated by her other side, also giving comfort, and I thought he must be an older son. As he turned his head to gaze at his suffering parents, I saw an expression of deep anguish on his face, and he appeared unable to speak for grief.

The hearing was over very quickly. The coroner merely said that the body had been identified, and a post-mortem examination was due to be carried out. The proceedings would therefore be adjourned for three days. Inspector Caldwell, leaning forward intently, grunted but made no comment, then sat back, and looked at his pocket watch. He showed no sign of leaving and I guessed that he had other cases to hear. The family rose to depart, and as they passed me, I saw nothing to change my judgement that they were Collier's parents and older brother. The only thing I had not seen before was that Mr Collier had a deeply sunken eye socket, with some scarring around it. It didn't do for me to stare at him too closely, especially under the circumstances, but on a quick glance, I thought that the ball of the eye was missing, either by accident or surgery.

On my way back to Barts I decided to go by way of the museum. It was still fully locked with the usual notices outside saying that it was closed for cleaning. There was no outward indication that anything remarkable had happened inside. On returning to my studies, I was welcomed with some heart-warming sympathy from my fellow students and one of the lecturers, who naturally assumed that I had attended an enquiry regarding a friend or relative. I took care not to enlighten them. One of the students was good enough to lend me his notes of the lecture I had missed, and I was very busy with making a copy for my own use and catching up on essential reading.

I had heard nothing more from Holmes throughout the day and was walking towards the chemistry laboratory late that afternoon when I saw ahead of me a tall man in rough workman's clothing going in the same direction. Despite the attire there was something about the gait that looked familiar, and I caught him up. 'Holmes, that is not at all your usual dress,' I said.

For some reason he looked a little offended to be recognised. I saw that he had gone to some trouble to change his appearance, as his normally well-groomed hair was rumpled and he had even applied a small goatee beard, the whole giving him something of a roguish look.

'I have been doing what a policeman cannot do,' he said. 'Even a plain clothes man is obviously a policeman by his manner and bearing, and will be officious in his questioning, and likely to meet some resistance. I have been to the docks offering my services as a winch man to discover what heavy items have been handled recently.'

'Have you discovered anything?'

'Nothing, only that the police have already been there. They have been searching for the wagon that transported the stone, but that too has not been seen. The stone may not be aboard a vessel, of course. There are any number of warehouses where it could have been concealed, assuming that it was taken to the docks at all. I am not as confident as the inspector on that point, but it is essential that all avenues must be explored. I will make another search tomorrow. But tell me about the inquest.'

I recounted as far as I could recall what had occurred, and he was especially interested in my description of the Collier family.

'Bury Street, yes I know it, running south from Great Russell Street, where one will find stationers, mantle makers and dairymen. Was any mention made of the employment of the deceased or the location of the incident?' Holmes asked.

'None whatsoever. Anyone not acquainted with the circumstances might easily have drawn the conclusion that Collier suffered an accident at his lodgings.'

'That was deliberate, I am sure. A thick veil of secrecy has been cast over the whole affair. Nothing should be revealed that could jeopardise the retrieval of the stone.' Holmes paused and gave a little cough. 'Stamford, you did well to see through my disguise. Might I ask — just as a matter of curiosity — what led you to identify me, despite all my pains to change my appearance?'

'Well, there are hardly any men of your height here that I know of, and there is your walk, which is very distinctive to those who know you, a kind of determined stride, I suppose.' I could see that he was giving my words deep consideration. 'Holmes,' I went on, 'I must ask, what did you mean yesterday, when you said that Dr Birch is a poor liar? He is a very respected man.'

Holmes smiled. 'He is, and I know nothing to his detriment. Incidentally, did you observe that though an Egyptologist he is fluent in Chinese but has never been to China?'

'I — no. I did glance at the books in his study, but none were in Chinese.'

'There were several in English which had been translated from the Chinese by Dr Birch.'

'Oh! I see. But how do you know he has never been there?'

'I may be wrong, but I have yet to meet a man who has been to China and does not have some souvenir of his travels about his person. As to his veracity, it was a compliment. I have no doubt at all that Dr Birch is honest and truthful by nature and so it was when he was compelled to conceal the truth from me, I observed that he became extremely uncomfortable. I am quite sure that the ransom note has secrets to reveal to which few men are party, and I am not of that number.'

'I don't think Inspector Caldwell will allow you to see it,' I said. 'But what do you think is being hidden?'

'A piece of paper with writing will hold a dozen clues the police may not see,' he said. 'But if I was to examine it, I would find them out.'

I was glad to see that his old confidence had returned. 'We may learn more when there is a second note,' I said. 'The one saying how to pay the ransom. It is a very large amount and I can't imagine how they propose it should be handed over.'

'Indeed. That is the crucial point. In cases of theft for ransom, the difficulty of stealing the item — even something as large and heavy as the Rosetta Stone — is as nothing compared with the safe receipt of the money. The theft is an unanticipated incident. The payment, however, has to be prearranged exactly as to time and place, which is known to both parties in the transaction. It is in vain for the thieves to insist that the victim must not employ the police because they almost always do, and when the time comes to hand over the ransom money, the police will be lying in wait to thwart them. That is the time of greatest danger to the criminal, when the arrest is most likely to be made. In this case it is doubly risky because the amount is large enough to have some bulk and weight to it. But this is an uncommon crime, and I sense an uncommon mind behind it, a puppet master of great wickedness and intelligence, a man who will stop at nothing, pulling the strings. He is the man we want.'

CHAPTER NINE

I well recall the chill of sheer terror that ran through me at Holmes' solemn pronouncement, and once again I was forced to wonder to what risks had I unwittingly exposed myself. I was not, I hasten to say, an utterly abject coward, although I was not and would never be of the stern stuff of which Watson was made. I gathered my courage and decided there and then, that if Holmes wanted me at his side for these dangerous adventures, I would not abandon him. Perhaps, I found myself thinking, it would even make me a better man.

'Do you know who this villain is?' I asked.

'No,' said Holmes, almost dreamily, his eyes seeming to gaze into a far distance, 'but I see his influence everywhere. In the newspapers which daily record the crimes of this land and of others, I often see the connections, the fine tendrils that link even the trivial with the audacious. Oh, such a man does not dirty his hands with committing the actual crimes, neither does he live in obvious opulence from the spoils. That is why he is never caught, never even suspected. He may appear on the surface to be quiet, unassuming, ascetic, his true nature wholly concealed from those about him. He can be identified by only a very few trusted lieutenants almost as evil but far less brilliant than he.' Holmes suddenly clenched his large hands into pale bony fists. 'But I will find him out. He may not know it yet, but I will.'

Holmes, as we have so often seen, had a very high opinion of his own abilities and rightly so, and a strong disdain for the commonplace. Only the most powerful opponents would feed his vanity, and during his busiest and greatest years, when he was partnered with Watson, he certainly encountered and defeated enough of them. But I believe it went much further than that.

Readers of Dr Watson's records of Holmes' later adventures, which I have no reason to doubt are an entirely accurate account of the events, cannot have failed to notice his friend's recurring obsession with uncannily powerful, supremely intelligent criminal masterminds. Recall if you will Holmes' description of the infamous Professor Moriarty, he of the large domed white skull indicating colossal brain power.

Looking back on that interlude, I am reminded that the only description we actually have of Moriarty is that provided by Holmes, both his appearance and demeanour. I do wish that Watson had met him, as I would have welcomed his more down to earth view of the man. I often feel sorry for Watson, who, as my readers will know, suddenly found himself swept into a madcap race across the continent fraught with the danger of imminent death, only to be faced with the apparent obliteration of his greatest friend. When I encountered Holmes in Montpellier some years later, I recall gently taxing him with this incident, but he told me nothing to illuminate it, indeed he utterly refused to discuss it. I was obliged at the time to treat that meeting with the utmost secrecy which of course I adhered to absolutely, although given the passage of many years, I plan to reveal the full circumstances later on in this memoir.

I am sometimes forced to wonder if Holmes' disappearance in 1891, leading to the period of his absence which is sometimes referred to by the students of his adventures as 'the hiatus', was in reality simply an escape from the great burdens placed upon him. He was by then so famous that he was assailed on all sides by the great and the noble offering him large sums of money to solve all their most important delicate and complicated affairs. He may have been on the verge of a breakdown of both his physical health and his nerves, a fate that he could only prevent by creating a general belief in his death. Notice the care with which he prepared Watson for his supposed death, softening what he knew would be a cruel blow to his loyal associate by hinting that it would be worth losing his life if it meant success in this mission. Notice his choice of location of the Reichenback Falls in the Swiss Alps for the final confrontation with his enemy, one where it would not be thought strange that no body was found yet demonstrated the inevitability of his demise.

He was also a lover of the dramatic gesture and had therefore determined to go out in a blaze of glory as the destroyer of a supremely powerful evil. To this end he might even have created the monster that was Professor Moriarty. Or did Holmes simply exaggerate a reality? But that is just my musings, and of course I could be completely mistaken, and all occurred exactly as described in Watson's memoirs, which trusted to the veracity of Holmes' account. We will never know the truth of the matter.

'Are you very busy tomorrow, Stamford?' Holmes asked, suddenly.

'There is nothing I cannot postpone,' I replied.

'Good. If you have suitable clothing for such an expedition, I would welcome a companion on my second search for the wagon and hopefully its contents. Another pair of eyes is always a good thing.'

'But you see everything, Holmes,' I said, lightly.

He recognised my gentle jest with a smile. 'I see, I observe, I deduce,' he said, 'but I am not infallible.'

CHAPTER TEN

Early the next morning, with both of us in the plainest workaday clothes we had, which was not a difficult requirement for a medical student, we set out on our search. I had to wonder how Holmes imagined that two men could succeed in a mission where the police with their greatly superior numbers had not, and although I feared offending him, I dared say as much. Fortunately, he was more amused than offended.

'Inspector Caldwell imagines that he is very clever to have spotted a clue in the thieves' note,' said Holmes, 'but given their detailed planning and what they have already achieved, would they then have been so careless as to tell him where to look? Following my earlier endeavours, I am more than ever of the opinion that the threat to drop the stone into the sea is nothing more than a deliberate misdirection, leading him to believe that the stone is on board a ship. They have drawn a red herring across the scent, and the inspector has decided to pursue it.'

'That is like the way they put the jar of smoke on the first floor to draw the attendants away from the theft from the ground floor,' I said.

'Precisely. My enquiries yesterday soon eliminated any possibility of the stone being aboard a vessel. Moreover, I discovered no evidence of a consignment of its size and weight arriving at the docks on a wagon. So neither is it in a warehouse there. This allowed me to concentrate my energies on finding where the thieves had procured the wagon, so I have been visiting businesses that hire out heavy goods transport. Many of these are situated by the dockside, and these I have now eliminated. But there are others, and I have identified them. The newspapers carry advertisements which are highly informative.'

'There must be businesses of that kind all over London,' I said, concerned at the enormity of the task Holmes was undertaking.

'There are, but we will begin with the carriage repositories close to Bloomsbury and work outwards. There, I feel, we will not see the footprints of Inspector Caldwell.'

It was as well that we were both young and vigorous, as it was a gruelling expedition. I had some difficulty in keeping up with Holmes' long eager strides, as we went from one carriage yard to another, asking whether they provided transport for heavy items which required a windlass. We were shown a number of goods wagons but on making enquiries were able to establish that none of the ones of the right size and robustness had been hired out on the day of the theft.

We stopped for a simple luncheon at a dining room, Holmes looking despondent but not about to give up.

'I have been wondering,' I said. 'It feels to me that there is something almost mathematical in their misdirection. Like the opposite points of the compass. The pot of smoke which not only distracted the attendants but was distant enough to give the thieves the time they needed to carry out their plans. The ransom letter pointed the police enquiries to the south of Bloomsbury, and the docks. But supposing they have taken the stone north?'

'That is a worthwhile observation, and it would be in keeping with their methods,' agreed Holmes. He mused on this for a few moments. 'A mathematical mind, yes. Again, I sense the influence of a highly intelligent opponent. We are not far from one of the great termini of the world, where goods of all kinds arrive and go from London. Once we have refreshed ourselves, we will continue our search.'

We were then in the region of Farringdon and determined to bend our steps northwards in the direction of Kings Cross. We had no map to guide us, but I had the impression that Holmes needed none, or if he did have one it was imprinted in his mind.

As we walked up together Holmes was amusing himself with a little game in which he attempted to identify the occupations and histories of passers-by simply by noting aspects of their appearance. He took account of the smallest signs such as most observers would not have seen, or if seen, would not have made the basis for deduction; the pattern of wear on trouser knees, the length of a stride, dust marks on toecaps, all these were significant and a valuable source of information. I made some attempt at matching him in this diversion but of course with indifferent results since I was too often in error, something he always liked to point out in some detail. When he explained it to me, I could only agree that he was correct as the answer became plain before my eyes. I realised of course that to Holmes it was not a game, it was a means of exercising his brain. When I complimented him, he said with a little smile, 'Oh, it is really nothing at all. If I told you all my methods, you would think them very ordinary indeed, quite unremarkable, such that anyone with a little diligence might achieve.'

'There is nothing ordinary and unremarkable about you, Holmes,' I said. I saw him warm to the compliment. It is perhaps one of his few faults that he liked flattery and enjoyed the sense that his superior abilities had been noted and appreciated.

There was more than one wagon hire business to examine, and at first none of our enquiries bore fruit, however we at last found one with rather more extensive premises than some of the others, J Dale, Horse and Carriage Repository, near to the railways. We walked under a wrought-iron archway with the name of the concern painted in tall lettering on a sheet metal sign and entered a cobbled yard busy with the movement of animals and carriages. We saw only one commercial wagon which was rather too small to interest us, but the yard was only the forecourt of a capacious shed with a high roof. We entered, seeing more vehicles drawn up which we started to inspect.

As we looked about us, a man in robust but shabby garments approached. He was not bearded but unshaven, his hands deeply grimed, and he smelled of oil and horses, yet his general air told us at once that he was the master of the business. He wore a long overcoat with deep pockets well stuffed with rolls of paper and folded leather-bound notebooks. A striped waistcoat bristled with pencils, and a heavy chain draped across his stomach suggested the presence of a substantial timepiece.

'Mr Dale?' asked Holmes.

'That's me, what can I do for you?'

'We are seeking a goods wagon for hire. It must be fitted with a strong windlass. Do you have such a thing?'

'I do,' he said. 'Come this way.'

I am not sure how either of us felt when we realised that we had at last found what we were looking for. I did my best to conceal my excitement and glanced at Holmes who looked as impassive as ever.

The wagon we were shown was not only of the right size, and fitted with a strong windlass in good condition, but as well as the sacking, ropes and tarpaulins one might have expected to find piled on the back there was a bundled heap of dirty carpets, ones which had seen better days and now only served as wrappings to protect fragile cargoes.

'When was this last hired out?' asked Holmes. 'I ask because my master said he saw such a wagon as this quite recently. It was just what he wanted, and he told me to look for one like it.'

Mr Dale pulled a roll of soiled papers from his pocket, and after opening it up with great solemnity and concentration was able to inform us that the wagon had been hired out only a few days ago. It was the date we knew to be the afternoon of the theft. It had been returned early the following morning.

'Then this might be the very one he saw,' said Holmes.

He leaped nimbly aboard the back of the wagon, and as he pulled aside the carpeting, I could not restrain a gasp. Underneath the pile was not more carpeting but a large wooden packing case.

'Were these carpets and the packing case on the wagon before it was hired out?' asked Holmes. He smelled the carpeting and wrinkled his nose in disgust.

'No,' said Dale, 'but then the hirers often do leave old packaging behind if they don't need it. I think all we provided was some sacking and a tarpaulin.'

Holmes pulled at the case, and the ease with which he moved it established that there was nothing of any weight inside. I suppose it was too much to hope that we might have found the Rosetta Stone in there. Lifting the lid, he inspected the contents, but after rummaging through them very thoroughly, found only straw. He took a measuring tape from his pocket, another recent purchase I assumed, and set about examining the interior of the case, the results of which he recorded in his notebook. He then used his pocket lens to study every aspect of the wagon, the floor of the bed, the exterior of the packing case, the windlass and the carpets, crawling about on his knees, agile as a cat.

The manager directed a curious look at me, and I could see he was wondering what Holmes was doing. 'His master is very particular,' I said.

'Halloa!' exclaimed Holmes suddenly, pointing to a fragment of paper protruding from between the planks of the wooden crate. 'There is a piece of a label here!' He leaned close to study it and as he did so, made a little exclamation, and allowed his nose to hover over the discovery. 'And a curious odour.' He beckoned to me. 'Come and let me have your opinion.'

Ignoring Mr Dale, who had thrust his hands into his pockets and was regarding us both with growing suspicion, I climbed up onto the wagon and sampled the smell arising from the crate, while Holmes took out his notebook and pencil and copied down the details from the label. I had expected him to prise the label away from the crate, but then I guessed that he believed the discovery to be of significance and had determined to leave it in position for the police to examine.

'Well?' he asked.

'There is a mixture of chemicals here,' I said, 'but the one that stands out is turpentine.'

'My thought, too,' he said.

'Do you think,' I asked, 'that the, er, consignment to be transported would fit inside this case?'

'The consignment,' he said, reading from his notebook, 'is forty-five inches long and twenty-eight and one half inches wide and eleven inches thick at its widest. I think it would just be possible, if it was aligned correctly.'

Holmes jumped down from the wagon and began a close examination of the wheels. 'Aha!' he uttered, 'as I had thought!' and used his penknife to take a sample of dry soil clinging to a wheel, placing his find into an envelope. He then approached the manager. 'Can you advise me what weight the windlass will lift? Would it perhaps raise something in the region of fifteen hundredweight to a ton in weight?'

Dale scratched his head. 'I've not tested it to its limit,' he said. 'It's a good windlass, that. Half a ton, no doubt. A ton seems like a lot but,' he shrugged, 'machinery can often surprise us.'

'Can you describe the man who last hired it?'

'I'm not sure what business that is of yours,' said Dale.

'None of mine, at all,' said Holmes, 'but it is my master's peculiarity to know who last used the wagons he hires. That is in case there should be any damage which is the fault of the previous hirers and for which he does not wish to be held responsible.'

Dale made a guttural sound and shook his head. 'Didn't give his name. Young man, that's all, paid in coin in advance. No quibble. That was all I needed to know. And there wasn't any damage when it came back, or I'd have seen it and charged for the repair. You have my word for that.'

'Did he specify what weight the windlass was to bear?'

'No, he just looked it over and said it was good for his purpose. Now enough of all these questions, let's talk business. Do you want to hire it or not?'

'Well, as long as the windlass is sound, I think I might have a customer for you,' said Holmes. 'Might I ask that you do not dispose of either the carpets or the packing case as they would be very useful. And if you have such a thing as a business card, please let me have one.'

We walked away, Holmes with a grubby card of J Dale Horse and Carriage Repository in his pocket. We were both in agreement that the wagon we had inspected was the one used to remove the stone from the museum.

'I estimate that the stone will fit in the packing case as long as the cradle and the glass case have been removed,' said Holmes. 'It would be useful if they could be found, as they must have been carried away, but I fear that the glass and its wood may simply have been destroyed, and the cradle could well have gone to a foundry by now. There is nothing useful to be learned from the carpeting, which judging by the dirt and its unpleasant odour must have been taken from a rubbish pile. I can state however that the windlass appears to have been used very recently, and the smears of dried soil on the wheels will, I believe, show that the wagon has been driven past the recent excavations on the Tottenham Court Road. But I will confirm that in the laboratory.'

'One thing I noticed was that the name of J Dale was painted on both sides of the wagon,' I said. 'The witnesses who saw the wagon that night never mentioned a name. At least they can't have done, or the police would have been there before us.'

'No, but they might have failed to observe it in the dark,' said Holmes. 'Or, since these thieves left little to chance, I think a piece of sacking or tarpaulin could have been used to conceal any lettering.'

'What will you do now?' I asked.

'The police must be notified, of course, and that would be best done through Dr Birch. I will pass this business card to him, and I expect Mr Dale will soon have a more searching visit than the one we made.'

'Was there anything of interest on the label?' I asked.

'It was a small piece with only partial wording,' he said. He took his notebook from his pocket, and I read 'rd & Co, 16' which Holmes told me had been printed, probably as a heading, and represented the partial name and address of a company, while inked below that, most likely indicating the contents, was 'Nectarin'. 'I think the packing case might once have been used by an importer of fruit. I cannot account for the odour of turpentine, other than its use as a cleaner. Of course, the packing case, too, might simply have been retrieved from a rubbish pile.'

It should have been a day of triumph at our discovery, but Holmes' mood was strangely muted. 'I fear,' he said, 'that since the wagon is lodged by a rail terminus, the stone may have been taken out of London. There has been enough opportunity to do so, and it might be anywhere by now, any farm with a hay barn or stables could house it. If it has been put in a fresh packing case it might be halfway to America. The wagon is a valuable clue, but I believe that more wide-ranging enquiries must now be a matter for the police force who are superior to us in numbers at least.'

'Is that the end of your enquiries?' I asked.

'Not in the slightest,' he said grimly, as we trudged back to the museum. 'I now have a somewhat delicate task to perform. I mean to extract the truth of the ransom note from Dr Birch.'

CHAPTER ELEVEN

As we walked, Holmes pointed out some of the places where he had been collecting samples of earth for detailed study in the laboratory, writing up descriptions and recording his results of his analyses. 'It ought to be possible,' he said, 'merely by examining the earth that clings to a boot to discover where the wearer has walked. Even in London the soils of different districts can be quite distinctive. I expect my studies of that subject alone to occupy several years.'

'I saw how much you learned from an examination of boot prints,' I said.

'Yes, the police make a great play of their use of boot prints, but they do not take it far enough. It is not merely a matter of matching a print to a suspect's boot. Even before they have their suspect the print could provide vital information that will reveal his identity. It is an important area that deserves further development.'

'I am sure your work will be of great assistance to the police,' I said.

'I doubt that they would thank me for it or even take my advice,' he replied. 'To them I am just an amateur meddler, a busybody who impedes rather than assists their enquiries.' He spoke lightly, carelessly, but I could sense his frustration.

It was a pair of rather dishevelled and very wearied explorers who finally arrived at the museum. Dr Birch took pity on us and conducted us to his apartments, asking us to stay for a supper of cold pie and beer. The family must already have eaten and left the gentlemen alone at the dining table and to their business. Our host was delighted at our discovery of the wagon, although like Holmes he remained despondent that the stone had still not been found and was dismayed at the prospect of it being beyond the means of anyone other than the thieves themselves to locate. Nevertheless, he agreed to inform the police of what we had found in the hope of better news. He called for a servant to bring paper, pen and ink, and wrote a note, enclosing the business card with it in an envelope. It was to be taken immediately to one of the policemen who were still on duty in the museum with instructions that it should be passed to Inspector Caldwell as a matter of urgency.

'I fear,' he said, 'that we will have no alternative but to pay the ransom after all. I spoke to Inspector Caldwell this morning and he as good as said so. He did suggest that we should offer to pay a lesser sum than the one demanded in the hope that the thieves would be content with that. Apparently, these criminals are often open to negotiation, and know that their initial demand will never be met. We have some funds, of course, but many expenses too, and there are important items that we are eager to acquire. I have been obliged to inform the museum trustees of our plight and they were deeply shocked as you can imagine. They may need to approach Parliament for assistance, but I am naturally concerned that any money we receive from that source will only go to reduce the amount of our annual grant, leaving us in dire need. The keepers have been in receipt of the same salary for quite some years and have started to make insistent applications for an increase. Caldwell did say that if we do pay the ransom, then once the stone is returned, he will do everything that is in his power to find the culprits and recover our funds, but I am not confident.'

Our supper was brought, and we fell to with an appetite. Our host did no more than sip a small glass of beer, although it failed to have the usual cheering effect that such a brew so often provides.

'Dr Birch,' said Holmes, pushing away his empty plate, 'can you advise me if you have received any further communication from the thieves?'

'Why no,' he said, 'just the first note they left.'

'Then you have not yet received instructions on how to pay the ransom?'

'No. I think they must realise that it would take us some little time to obtain the funds.'

'And of course, too much information given early would forearm the police,' said Holmes. 'If they knew how, where and when the ransom was to be paid, they would take action to apprehend the thieves. There would be a danger that you might never recover the stone.'

'That is very true.'

'But that would only occur if the police were to be told of it,' said Holmes, with slow deliberation in his voice.

Dr Birch looked a little startled. 'Do you mean that when I receive final instructions as to the ransom payment, I should not inform the police? That we should pay it and only tell them once it is done? Is that your advice?'

'I mean,' said Holmes, 'that you already know all the details of how the ransom is to be paid, and you are concealing the information.'

Birch stared at Holmes. His mouth opened and closed indecisively but he did not speak. If there had been any doubt in my mind about Holmes' deduction it vanished.

'As Inspector Caldwell said,' Holmes went on, confidently, 'and I trust his long experience on this point, it is most unusual for a ransom letter not to say how the payment is to be made or even to allude to the future provision of instructions. When you opened the envelope in front of Dr Martinson you did not show him the contents, but he told me that it was a folded sheet of writing paper and referred to it as a letter. Inspector Caldwell, however, described the disappointing contents as a "little note". I have had the feeling for some while that you are not telling me everything, and you display signs of discomfort every time the ransom letter and its contents are mentioned. Dr Birch, I am sure that you would not conceal anything from the police unless you were acting under the direst threat. I believe that there was more to that note, a section which you are concealing. A portion which you cut away and retained, leaving only the upper part.'

Dr Birch uttered a groan. 'You are right, of course. I was afraid that if I told the police, all would be lost!'

'I am not the police,' said Holmes, evenly.

'That is true,' said Birch, 'and you have acted in some ways better than they.' He threw up his hands. 'Yes, yes, I admit it, when I first saw the letter, I cut away the lower part and retained it, but once a man's life had been lost, I knew I could delay no longer. Inspector Caldwell now has the remaining portion. He was somewhat annoyed with me, but he understood my initial reluctance. He has, however, promised faithfully not to act upon its contents until we have the stone.'

'Might I enquire what it said?' asked Holmes.

Birch hesitated but only briefly. 'If I was to reveal to you what I know I will do so only if you promise by all that you hold dear, not to use or pursue the information or the result will be the most terrible catastrophe!'

'I promise to do nothing that would endanger the safe retrieval of the stone,' said Holmes, 'unless, of course, a life is at stake. Do you accept those terms?'

'I do. I must,' said Birch, sadly.

'I assume that the details of the ransom payment are currently only known to yourself, the inspector, and the museum trustees?'

'That is correct.'

'Go on.'

Birch looked at me, and for a moment I thought he was about to ask me to leave, but he did not. Perhaps he believed that anything he told Holmes I would learn soon afterwards in any case. This was not at all the position as far as I was concerned, but I did not seek to disabuse him.

'As you correctly surmised, the lower portion of the note provided instructions as to how the ransom was to be paid. It demanded that the money should be paid in full into an account held at Cook's Bank. Once this has been done, I am instructed to place a coded advertisement in *The Times*. The museum will then be sent a message to say where the stone is to be found. I have no doubt that the bank is quite unaware of the purpose for which this account has been opened and that by the time the message has been sent revealing the location of the stone, the funds will have been extracted.'

'Have you heard of Cook's Bank?' asked Holmes.

'I have heard it mentioned, but I know nothing of its operation,' said Birch. 'I believe it is a respectable establishment.'

'I can't say I have heard of it at all,' I replied.

'When I was at university, said Holmes, 'there was a fellow there, an idler without a thought in his head, whose father was extraordinarily wealthy. The father had sent him there in the hope of knocking some sense into him, a forlorn enterprise. However, this sprig liked to boast that his father banked at Cook's. Cook's Bank is the preserve of royalty, nobility and individuals of great substance. It provides complete confidentiality, the most perfect efficiency, and a security which is the envy of the world's greatest banking houses. It operates only through a few outwardly small and very ordinary looking establishments in some of the major cities of the world.'

'Then whatever we do, the culprits will never be found!' exclaimed Birch. 'What guarantee will we ever have of retrieving the stone, even if we accede to their demands!'

'None whatsoever,' said Holmes, bluntly. 'I am not sure if even Scotland Yard knows what it is dealing with. Inspector Caldwell's plan is a simple one, and it could well work if he was faced with a commonplace thief. He has advised that if you want to see the Rosetta Stone again, you should pay the ransom and then once the stone is safely recovered, the police will apprehend the criminals. But this is no commonplace thief. The police may well arrest some of the gang, the humble foot soldiers who were well paid for their role and their silence, but the mastermind behind it will not be found — his identity, his very existence never so much as suspected. I am also of the opinion that if the museum deposits the ransom money into that account you will never see the Stone again.'

CHAPTER TWELVE

On the following morning the inquest on young Henry Collier was resumed. I met with Holmes at the King's Head. Sensational cases often draw large crowds of press and public, and courts can be overwhelmed with demands for admission, but the strict secrecy about this case had ensured that there was only the usual attendance one might expect at any inquest. Had the true circumstances of Collier's death been known we would have had considerable difficulty in obtaining seats, or even gaining entry to the building.

Holmes was carrying a copy of that morning's *Times* and as we waited for the proceedings to commence, he scoured it carefully for any mention of the museum but was pleased to find none. One article caught his eye, however, and he prodded the paper to point it out. 'At least the police are efficient enough in some areas. I see that the poisoner Donaldson has been sentenced to hang.'

He had clearly been following the progress of that trial and I asked him about the case.

'Oh, he is a foul creature, and the world will be well rid of him. He poisoned his wife and children and sealed the bodies in a trunk, which he deposited in a warehouse, intending that they would never be found, and no doubt thinking himself very clever. When his crime was revealed he blamed it on his wife, declaring her to be both a murderess and a suicide. But the police discovered a letter he had written while his family was still living, in which he claimed to be a childless widower. His arrogance has condemned him.'

I often noticed Holmes taking a keen interest in some of the more remarkable crimes reported in the newspapers. As he elaborated on the chemical means Donaldson had used to prevent the odour of decomposition escaping from the trunk, it confirmed my supposition that this interest must have prompted his scientific studies. I could not see however that he could ever be employed as an analyst or be summoned to court as an expert witness as he had no desire to obtain a formal qualification.

When Collier's family arrived, I pointed them out to Holmes, who laid aside his newspaper and regarded them with his characteristic enquiring look. It was as if his eyes were a lantern casting illumination on the subjects that attracted his interest, the better for him to examine the details. No wonder people sometimes quailed under that gaze.

Inspector Caldwell bustled in and took a seat near to the witnesses' chair. I wondered what action he had taken on the information we had provided the previous day, and hoped that, as some small reward for our efforts, he might consent to enlighten us, or at the very least offer his thanks.

The jurymen took their seats and Dr Hardwicke, bearing a large bundle of papers, arrived to occupy the coroner's chair, and opened the proceedings. 'We will start with the resumed inquest on Henry Collier. I call my first witness, Dr Summerlee.'

The man who stepped forward was middle-aged, and rather brisk in his manner. His stomach was evidence of a good appetite, his expression that of a man who treated life and death as one, the exploration of the corpse of a murder victim being merely one incident in his daily work.

'Dr Summerlee,' asked Hardwicke, 'did you attend the deceased prior to his death?'

'I did. I was called to his home by the associate with whom he lodged, a Mr Robson, and was told that he had received a blow on the head which had rendered him briefly unconscious. The incident had already been reported to the police. There were no other injuries and Mr Collier was in good spirits, and able to converse normally. He said that the Robsons were looking after him very well and insisted that he required nothing in the way of medicine or even a bandage. There was no bleeding that I could see, and as far as I was able to observe the only sign was a small contusion which he said he did not wish to have touched. I said that if there was any change in his condition I should be called again.

'On the following day I was sent for as a matter of urgency. I found him very much declined, with severe headaches, dizziness, vomiting, and blood and other fluid draining from one ear. There had clearly been an injury to the brain with bleeding inside the skull, yet from the exterior, all that was visible was an area of bruising. He passed away later that day.'

'Did you carry out the post-mortem examination?'

'I did. The deceased was a healthy and well-nourished individual aged twenty-two. The only external injury was a contusion on the temple —' Summerlee briefly turned to face the inquest jury and pointed to the location on his own head, just above his left ear — 'which was undoubtedly caused by contact with a hard object. Given the size and shape of the bruise I have come to the conclusion that it was not an accident as might have occurred from a fall in which one might strike the head on a surface such as a floor, or something resembling the edge of a table, but was the result of contact with some kind of weapon, something with a rounded end.

'It was not, however, a very hard blow. It is possible that he was in movement at the time — perhaps he saw the blow coming and tried to avoid it, which would have greatly reduced its force. In any other man it would not have been fatal or even serious. The deceased, however, was singularly unfortunate in that the bones of his skull were abnormally thin in that area. My examination revealed a fracture of the skull and an accumulation of blood in the brain which eventually led to his death. The fact that when he was found he was conscious and lucid led to the understandable belief that he had not suffered a serious injury and would recover with rest. I have no difficulty in concluding that the blow on the head was the sole cause of death.'

Hardwicke looked at his notes again before he continued. 'Dr Summerlee, you are aware of course that a second individual was the victim of a similar incident at the same time, but he is thought to be on the way to recovery. Were you able to examine that individual's injury and compare it to the blow suffered by the deceased?'

'I was, and I found that the size and shape of the injury to the deceased, even though it made a small imprint on the scalp, is very similar indeed to that suffered by the other victim. His injury was in a different part of the skull.' Once again for the benefit of the jury, Summerlee pointed to the place, which was at the back of his head and rather nearer to the right side than the left. 'The bone there was very much thicker than in the case of the deceased. While I am not able to say conclusively that they were caused by the same implement, I am of the firm opinion that they were inflicted either by the same or a very similar object.'

'Can you describe what that object might have been?'

'Yes. I have seen injuries of this kind before. It would have been something like a club or a walking stick, quite probably with the bulbous end drilled out and filled with lead. It is a weapon often employed by criminals or carried by gentlemen as a means of defending themselves against crime. I cannot of course comment on the motive for either assault.'

Dr Hardwicke had no further questions for Summerlee and thanked him for his report. Summerlee looked eager to leave but was asked to remain in case there were any further questions, and he sat down with a rather ill-grace.

'I now call Inspector Caldwell of Scotland Yard,' said Dr Hardwicke.

Caldwell strode up to give evidence. Even when seated he liked to square his shoulders and give every impression of a man not to be trifled with.

'Inspector,' began Hardwicke, 'I understand that there are aspects of this incident which are currently under investigation by the police, which for very prudent reasons are not to be generally reported, and do not in any case have any importance for the verdict of this inquest.'

'That is so,' said Caldwell. 'Our enquiries are not to be compromised.'

'I trust that the press men here present will take due notice,' said Hardwicke, giving the assembled reporters a very firm stare.

Inspector Caldwell smiled. 'Or I might be having a word with them myself. You have been warned, sirs.'

'Has a weapon been recovered?'

'Not yet, but we are confident that it will be.'

'Is the second victim making a good recovery?'

'He is under close medical supervision, and it is believed that he will recover. He is unfortunately unable to give any account of what occurred.'

'Are the police of the opinion that the deceased and the other victim had both been assaulted by another individual, or more than one?' asked Hardwicke. 'I am seeking confirmation that one of the men did not in your opinion, assault the other.'

'Our enquiries have shown that the two men were on good terms and there had never been any quarrel or disagreement between them,' replied Caldwell. 'The weapon does not appear to have been removed by anyone we have interviewed, and we believe that it was carried away by the assailant.'

Hardwicke thanked the inspector. As Caldwell returned to his seat, he saw Holmes and me in the gathering and gave us an extremely disapproving look. I suppose I ought to have expected that. Even though we had been the agents of valuable information I thought it must have put his nose out of joint to be told that he had been following a false trail.

Hardwicke completed his notes and addressed the jury. 'In these proceedings we are concerned with the cause of death although where the proximal cause is violence, the jury is entitled to pronounce on whether death is misadventure, or the result of a crime. We have heard that two men were assaulted with a weapon most probably of the type described by Dr Summerlee, a weapon which was not found at the scene. It appears very unlikely indeed that there was any kind of violence between the men. It follows that the deceased was not assaulted by the second victim but by an unknown individual.

'That individual may not have intended to kill the deceased; indeed, we have learned from Dr Summerlee that death was an unfortunate consequence of the composition of the deceased's skull which the assailant might have known nothing about. But it cannot be disputed that a person who strikes another on the head with a weighted club has every intention of causing him harm. At the very least he means to stun him. It may well be that he cares nothing as to the amount of harm he inflicts. If the man dies therefore, then the attacker who has committed an act of malice, may be charged with murder. The jury should now consider its verdict. Gentlemen, you may retire if you wish.'

The jury men filed solemnly into a side room for their deliberations, and possibly also refreshments.

'The next case on my list,' said Hardwicke, 'is likely to occupy some time and I will therefore adjourn briefly to await the verdict on the first case before commencing it.'

One or two people rose to stretch their legs. The Collier family made no move, and I saw the mother clutching a large handkerchief to her eyes and being comforted. It must have been something of an ordeal to hear of her son's last hours. Since no member of the family had been called as a witness, I guessed that they had not been able to be with him when he breathed his last.

'I doubt we will have to wait long,' said Holmes. 'Ah, here comes the inspector for a word.' My companion was not able to restrain a smile of triumph. 'He looks very displeased.'

Inspector Caldwell was approaching, and since we were both seated, he took the opportunity to loom mightily above us. I sensed that looming was something he did often. 'A word in your ear, Mr Holmes,' he said, gruffly. He did not expect opposition.

Holmes rose and followed him to one side of the room. I stood, too, but Caldwell turned and snapped, 'Not you! I think you ought to know better and choose your friends better too. I can see who is holding the reins here.'

I sat down again, but not in my original seat. I chose one nearby so I could hear what Caldwell was saying.

Standing face to face, Holmes was taller than Caldwell by several inches, but he declined to use this to his advantage, and stood leaning forward intently.

'Now then,' Caldwell began, 'this is a word of warning to you, Mr Holmes. I want to make this very clear. The police don't mind receiving information from members of the public. It can be extremely useful, although sometimes it can simply be a waste of our valuable time. But what we don't want is people like you, who think they are cleverer than the police, acting like detectives out of a cheap storybook. Police work is police work, and it is not for the public. Now I don't know how you got started on this or why you have decided to interfere. If you are employed to assist Dr Birch in his work, that is all well and good, but I have told Dr Birch that that is as far as it should go. If I should find you impeding police enquiries once more, I shall have no hesitation in having you placed under arrest. Do you understand?'

Holmes was deadly calm. Had he been roused to anger he would not have been so frightening or so impressive as he was when holding himself under iron control. 'I trust,' he said, icily, 'that the information concerning the wagon was of some use to you?'

'No Mr Holmes, it was not!' snapped Caldwell. 'We know that the purloined item was taken to the docks. All the evidence points to it. Yet you go gallivanting about lighting on some wagon north of here. With a windlass that can barely even lift half a ton!'

'How do you know that?' asked Holmes.

'Well, you see, that is what good police work does, it looks at all the facts. Not that you would know about that. We did talk to the owner of wagon, and of course he remembered your visit and all the funny business playing at being a detective and asking him about the windlass and Lord knows what. So he wondered how much it would really lift, and after you went he tested it. It was good for half a ton, no more. I can assure you

Mr Holmes that that wagon can't have been the one we are looking for.' He shook a stout finger in Holmes' face. 'Now, let that be a lesson to you.'

At that moment the jury began to file back, and we resumed our seats. I glanced at Holmes but said nothing. He was deadly pale, but there were little touches of red on his cheekbones.

'Have you reached a verdict?' asked Dr Hardwicke.

The foreman stood. 'We have. Our verdict is that Henry Collier was murdered by some person or persons unknown.'

'I concur,' said Hardwicke. He thanked the jury and announced the next case. Caldwell remained to hear it and we took our leave.

CHAPTER THIRTEEN

It was a largely silent and thoughtful journey as we made our way back to Barts. We hardly spoke except to comment on the inevitability of the verdict, and Caldwell was not mentioned at all. I decided not to ask Holmes, but I had to assume that this incident would mark the end of his involvement in the case, and that he would henceforward be obliged to leave the investigation in the hands of the police. When we reached the hospital, we parted ways, Holmes to continue his chemistry work, I to another lecture.

That afternoon I was surprised to receive a visit from George Luckhurst. He was looking less agitated than before, although he clearly had a great many unhappy concerns on his mind. I noticed at once that he was wearing a black cravat, and there was a band of black crape around his hat, but in view of our short acquaintance I did not feel entitled to make an enquiry as to his recent bereavement. He saw my look of sympathy and understood.

He was hoping to speak to Holmes, and we looked for him in the chemistry laboratory, the dissecting room, the students' library and the reading room, but as was so often the case he was nowhere to be found and no-one had any idea where he was. I felt very sorry for Luckhurst as he seemed like a good sort of fellow, someone who cared a great deal about others, and was sorely pressed by anxieties not of his own making. I suggested that we take a bite to eat at a nearby dining room, and he readily agreed, though it soon became apparent that he had no appetite, and instead drank a great deal of coffee.

'Since I was in London, I had hoped to see my uncle again,' he said, 'but when I advised him of my proposed visit, I received a note from him saying that it might be best for the time being if I did not come to the museum, as it is closed and there was a great deal of work being done. I appreciate that of course, but somehow, I feel sure that something is not right, something he is afraid to tell me. Do you know if Holmes discovered anything more about the visions?'

I was in a difficult position as might be imagined and was obliged to choose my words carefully. 'Holmes has made some enquiries, and we both think that you need not be concerned about your uncle's health. I did not notice anything about his eyesight which suggested that he requires an examination. Neither do I believe that he has drained his energies from overwork. Far from it, he is engaged in studies which he finds very stimulating and is shortly expecting a delegation of renowned experts to discuss his findings. We have concluded that a possible answer to the mystery is that he may simply have seen some visitors to the museum who had lost their way in the fading light. Dr Birch has said as much. Either that or there are optical effects which in certain lighting conditions will occur in even the healthiest systems.'

'But why am I not to pay him a visit?' asked Luckhurst, plaintively. 'He has never put me off before.'

'I can only guess that it might be something to do with the cleaning and repair work currently being done,' I said. 'Perhaps you could see him next week, when the museum re-opens.'

There was a long silence then Luckhurst said, 'I have just come from the deathbed of my great-aunt. I received a telegram this morning informing me that she had passed away and I came to pay my respects.'

'I am sorry — were you very close?'

He bit his lip, and his eyes watered a little. 'I was extremely fond of her and I think she was of me. I saw her whenever I could. She was the sister of my paternal grandfather, and a courageous lady who had been an invalid for a number of years. I last saw her on the day after we first met. She was then as clear in her mind as she had always been, and we spoke of family affairs. I happened to mention that my uncle had been experiencing some difficulties with his eyesight and to my surprise she asked me if he had been drinking. I replied that he never drank, but she told me that in his younger days he had been rather addicted to it. In fact, she said that was the reason his engagement was broken off. Both the young lady and her parents were of the Society of Friends and although she loved him dearly, she could not tolerate the habit, and asked to be released from her promise. I know that my uncle is an abstainer now, but do you think — is there any possibility that he might have turned to it again?'

'I was not looking for it when I saw him, of course,' I said. 'Perhaps it was the loss of the lady's love that made him take the pledge. But now I think about it, I saw no sign of it at all. In fact, he took great pains to tell us that he was an abstainer and had only drunk cocoa on the night of the curious event. He was quite upset at any suggestion that he might have been intoxicated.'

'I have never seen any sign of it either,' agreed Luckhurst. 'Will you tell Holmes what I have said, and if he has anything to add to his previous observations will he write to me?' He handed me a card. 'Or if he cannot, might you write?'

'Of course,' I said.

He drained his coffee cup, thoughtfully. 'Your friend Holmes is a very interesting fellow,' he said.

'He is,' I agreed.

'Have you known him very long?'

'No, we have only recently met as we are fellow students. I really hardly know him at all. But in that short acquaintance I have come to believe that he has a brain unlike that of any man I have ever met. He is wholly devoted to science and logic.'

Luckhurst seemed to have drawn some comfort from our conversation, and we made our goodbyes and parted, he to his studies and I to mine.

Later that day I was working in the students' library when the librarian approached and beckoned me to the front desk. Conversation between the students in the library was not permitted, and he whispered, 'You have a visitor. He is waiting outside.' I glanced out of the door and saw Dr Martinson in the corridor. He looked hollow eyed and anxious. I nodded to the librarian, and quickly collected my papers. As I left, one or two of the other students glanced up, exchanged looks, shook their heads, and went back to their work.

'Mr Stamford,' whispered Martinson confidentially, 'I don't suppose I could trouble you to come to the museum? I have left a note for Holmes at his lodgings and his landlady says he has not been there all day, and I had hoped to find him here and asked everyone I could find, but no one has seen him.'

I was glad for Holmes' sake, and also for my own that Martinson was so quietly dressed and respectable in appearance otherwise his earnest search might have raised some eyebrows. No one would have taken him to be a debt collector or a law officer about to serve a summons. I have to confess that as he was speaking so very close to me, I did check for any odour of alcoholic beverages, and reassuringly found none.

'Unless of course you can tell me where he might be?' he added hopefully.

'I am afraid not, he is a something of a law unto himself,' I replied, 'but I do know that he has been out a great deal pursuing enquiries on your behalf, and his findings have been turned over to the police. If he has anything further to report, he will come straight to the museum.'

'Yes, Dr Birch has instructed the attendants that he is to be allowed admittance. Will you come, Mr Stamford?'

Naturally I agreed to go with him, and we were soon aboard a cab driving up to Montague Place. I was curious as to the reason for his urgent appeal. He soon enlightened me.

'Dr Birch told me that when Mr Holmes made an examination of the workshop after the theft, he noticed that there was damage to the larger of our heavy barrows,' he said. 'This was in perfect accord with the police theory that the stone was removed on that barrow which was equal to carrying the weight and also the evidence of witnesses who saw the removal taking place. The thing is —' he sighed — 'I really don't know what to think now. A Mr Philips came to the museum today; he is one of the general repair men we call in from time to time. He said that he had come to replace the wheel attachment on the barrow as there was a crack in the metal.'

'That would be the damage that Holmes observed,' I said.

'Precisely, yes, that was my first thought. But the thing is, he said that he was asked to do this by Davis, the workshop manager last week. That was *before* the theft. Davis came in today as well, and he confirmed this.'

'Perhaps last week there was just a small crack which was made worse by transporting the stone,' I suggested.

'No,' said Martinson with a weary shake of the head. 'Davis has looked at the barrow and he is adamant that it appears exactly as it did when he ordered the repair. I was really hoping that Holmes could come and speak to him, and make some observations, but…'

'I will do my best,' I promised. 'Have the police been called?'

'I expect so.'

I recalled that I had already been introduced to the police as Dr Birch's assistant, and decided that if Inspector Caldwell was there, I would have to continue in that guise until I had the opportunity of asking any questions of my own. I had a notebook and pencil about me, although as I checked my pockets for them, I found a medical monograph and transferred it to an interior pocket as it seemed an unlikely thing for a student of Oriental antiquities to be carrying. When we arrived, I saw that the cleaners were at work again.

'They have all been interviewed,' said Martinson, 'and every one of them can prove an alibi for the time of the theft. The police are satisfied that none of them had anything to do with it. Philips and Davis also, are trusted men, and have been cleared of any involvement.'

I felt sure that Holmes would want to examine their boots but said nothing.

We peered into the workroom where Sergeant Lestrade, notebook in hand, was deep in discussion with two men I had not seen before, and whom I assumed were the repair man and the workshop manager. At one point all three crouched down to study the wheels of the larger of the two heavy barrows, then there were some comments on the smaller one, with one of the men pointing out the state of the wheels. Finally, Lestrade rose to his feet and made some notes. Dr Birch was present, but he said nothing and merely listened to the conversation.

One of the cleaners, a shock-headed fellow with a crooked back wearing a large apron tied about his thin body and rough gloves was perched high on a ladder scouring the upper casements. Looking at him with a medical eye I could not help noticing the remarkable strength and flexibility about his arms and shoulders despite the apparent distortion of his body.

'Let us go in and see what we can learn,' I whispered to Martinson and we entered.

CHAPTER FOURTEEN

I greeted Dr Birch and made some excuse for my presence. I think I said I was making a tally of some sort and I proceeded to study the shelves of bottles, pretending to inspect the contents and make notes.

'Well, that is all I have to ask for now,' said Lestrade. 'I shall write a report and I have no doubt that you will be receiving a visit from Inspector Caldwell very soon. In fact, he might already be on his way.' He put his notebook into his pocket, and on noticing me, gave me a very hard look before hurrying away.

'Did you not find Holmes?' Birch asked Martinson.

'I couldn't locate him, but I have left a note at his lodgings,' said Martinson. 'Mr Stamford kindly agreed to come.'

Birch sighed. He didn't have to say it, but I appreciated that I was not a worthy substitute. 'Well Mr Stamford, we hardly know what to believe now. It seems there is some difficulty with our understanding of how the stone was removed. Mr Davis our workshop manager noticed last week that our large barrow was in need of repair and asked Mr Philips to come in and attend to it.'

'I told the sergeant,' said Philips, a burly fellow in his forties who looked as if he had been born with a spanner in his hand, 'I said to him, that if you were to go and put something on this barrow fifteen hundredweight or more, then it would collapse, and then you wouldn't be able to move it at all. But he wasn't having it. Said it must have been used a couple of days ago as it was seen being used. So I said it might have been used for a lighter weight, I estimate it would have taken maybe five hundredweight, it's a good solid vehicle this, but not fifteen. Then he asked if the smaller one was all right, and it is all right, as you can see, but if you'd tried putting fifteen hundredweight on it then it wouldn't be all right at all. Look at the wheels and the axles. Does that look like a vehicle that has been overloaded? I don't think so.'

'Then,' said Davis, with an air of quietly pained regret, 'he tried to tell us that the large barrow might not have been so bad when I called in Mr Philips, and that perhaps there had been just a little crack so it could have been used and the crack just got to the size it is now because of it. I was obliged to tell him that I know what I saw and last week it was the same as it is now.' He glanced around to see if anyone else would call his judgement into question. No-one did.

'In other words,' said Holmes, suddenly appearing beside me, discarding the shock wig and unwinding the strings of the grubby apron, 'the police theory of how the stone left the building is wholly exploded, and we must think of something else.'

Birch and Martinson looked quite amazed at his abrupt materialisation, and I suppose I did my best to look surprised, although I had already deduced where Holmes was to be found.

'You have been here all this while!' exclaimed Martinson. 'I looked everywhere for you!' He sat down very suddenly.

'There there, poor fellow, I will try not to startle you again,' said Holmes with a smile. 'I must apologise to you gentlemen for my little diversion, I thought I might hear more than I might otherwise have done if I adopted a simple disguise. I may need it again if Caldwell arrives soon.'

Birch merely shook his head in amused wonderment.

'But something did leave the building on a barrow,' I said, 'unless the witnesses are mistaken or untruthful.'

'Was anything due to be removed that day?' asked Birch. 'We were told that it was thought by one witness that some carpets were being taken to be cleaned.'

'Nothing at all,' said Davis, firmly, 'or I would have known about it.'

'But now I am more concerned than ever,' said Birch. 'We thought we knew that the stone had been taken away, most probably to the docks, and now it seems that we know nothing at all.'

At that moment, Holmes quickly replaced his wig and wrapped himself about in the apron. I heard footsteps approaching and realised that he had identified the characteristic purposeful stride of Inspector Caldwell. By the time Caldwell was in the room, Holmes was halfway up the ladder, his distorted back shrinking his distinctive height by several inches.

'Ah, Dr Birch, what is all this about the broken barrow?' said Caldwell. 'I encountered my sergeant on the way here and he apprised me of the situation.'

Between them, Dr Birch, Mr Davis and Mr Philips made their case for the impossibility of either of the heavy barrows having been used to remove anything weighing fifteen hundredweight, while Dr Martinson simply looked unhappy. At first, Caldwell tried waving away the objection. True to his character as Holmes had stated, I saw that the stronger the contrary case was raised, the more entrenched in his original theory the inspector became. Dr Birch, after his mildly made explanations, abandoned the struggle and left the hard work to Davis and Philips. With their skill and experience they felt themselves more than qualified to disagree with a policeman, which they did, fearlessly.

'But the fact remains,' said Caldwell, at last, 'that there are witnesses, two gentlemen who saw a laden barrow leave the building. If it was not one of these here, then it must have been another one. They might have come prepared and brought their own on the wagon.'

'Was there a witness to that?' asked Birch. 'I rather thought from our conversation the other day that there was a witness who saw the wagon drive up and there was no equipment on it other than the windlass.'

Caldwell scowled and pulled his notebook from his pocket, thumbing rapidly through it with a noticeable air of irritation. 'Here it is,' he announced, 'five witnesses in all. Two gentlemen who saw the barrow with its load being wheeled out. They said two men or perhaps three men did this; one man was standing on the wagon and another holding the horses. Then there was a lady who saw what she thought was a bundle of carpets being lifted aboard the wagon from the barrow by windlass. She saw four men, or possibly five or six, she couldn't remember. One was holding the horses, one or two standing on the wagon, and one or possibly two helping to guide the load aboard. Another lady, her sister, they were walking together, saw something very similar. Then —' he turned the page and smiled. 'Yes, here we have it. The one witness who saw a wagon fitted with a windlass draw up outside the museum. He said that one man was driving, one sat beside the driver, and there were five sitting in the back. Says the wagon was unladen apart from sacking and the like.' Caldwell chuckled. 'Witness was a boy of twelve. So I think that decides that. No, I think we will find that either the thieves brought their own barrow or the one you have there is a lot stronger than you think it is.'

Davis and Philips did not look pleased with that conclusion. 'I'll get on with the repair then,' said Philips, and opened a bag of tools.

'Inspector,' said Martinson, 'I don't suppose you have any news for us?'

'Not yet,' said Caldwell. 'Now if you'll excuse me, I need to get on. We've narrowed our field of operations so we may have something for you soon.'

Once the inspector was gone Holmes re-joined us.

'What about you, Mr Holmes?' asked Martinson. 'Please tell us you have made some progress.'

'I have not located the stone,' said Holmes, 'but when we sweep away untenable theories we are left with a clearer vision. We must start with first principles and incontrovertible facts. The stone was here and now it is not. We only have to understand how this was achieved and then we will know where it is.'

'What astonishes me,' I said, 'is how the Egyptians were able to move such large things, especially those great monuments. Did they have cranes and hoists as we do?'

'They had something of the kind for water and goods, but not enough to lift great stones,' said Martinson. 'We believe that large sculptures and building blocks were drawn on sledges by slaves. They had great numbers of slaves. Other ancient civilisations with more abundant supplies of hardwood might have used logs as rollers, but in the desert the Egyptians had only the sweat and lives of many men.'

'I have a question for Mr Davis, if I may,' said Holmes.

Davis looked surprised, but Birch reassured him that this was in order.

'I have been admiring your display of African sunbirds,' said Holmes. 'Can you advise me where they were purchased?'

'We obtain all our specimens from Ward's of Piccadilly,' said Davis, a little surprised at the question. Holmes simply thanked him.

'I have learned a singular lesson today,' said Holmes, as we left the workroom. 'If I had paid more attention when Martinson gave me the tour of the building before the theft, I might have noted the condition of the barrow. As it was, I did not.'

'But at the time,' I reminded him, 'Dr Martinson was mainly troubled by the possible threat to the gold. Had that been stolen one man might have carried it. There was no reason for you to pay special attention to the barrows.'

'My method is to pay attention to everything,' said Holmes, irritably, 'however small, however unimportant it might seem at the time. No, I have failed in this instance. It makes me wonder what other failures I might have committed. Too many, I fear.'

'What did you learn during your masquerade?' I asked.

'The occupation of window cleaner is generally dull but full of possibilities. One's presence is largely ignored which is a great benefit. Little did Inspector Caldwell suspect just now that he was providing me with the statements of the witnesses. He would not have done so had he known I was listening. I did have the chance of examining the boots of the cleaners and saw nothing to suggest that they had entered the workroom after blood was spilled. And Mr Philips and Mr Davis are also in the clear.'

'And your question concerning the sunbirds?'

'When I was cleaning in the workroom, I happened to notice the museum's label for the display — their Latin name is *Nectarinia*. I have some further facts to assemble, but if I am correct the packing crate we found on the wagon at Mr Dale's was taken from the museum workshop.'

'I must admit,' I confessed, 'that I thought after Inspector Caldwell told you to back off you would not pursue the mystery anymore. I am glad that you do go on with it because I am not pleased with his manners or his methods.'

Holmes smiled. 'But the inspector does have his uses. He serves to show me the way. He lights up the flaws in his arguments like a lantern by following them so strongly. He is indispensable.'

'Do you think you can discover how the stone was moved?'

'Once Dr Martinson has recovered his strength, which has been sorely tested, I will speak to him again on the subject of the Egyptians. I have an instinct that the answer to all our questions lies with them, but even he does not know it.'

I was obliged then to tell Holmes about my conversation with George Luckhurst and what his great-aunt had revealed. Holmes agreed that Martinson showed no signs of having fallen back to his old habits, although he observed that a man's past might carry many ghosts to torment him.

CHAPTER FIFTEEN

As we left the museum, I found that Holmes was determined to linger awhile in Montague Place. It was a quiet and very respectable location. In those days there was a terrace of well-kept houses fronted by tall iron railings securely gated, with steps leading down to enclosed basement areas. Some had side alleys leading to rear gardens. If on the night of the robbery, thieves had lurked in the dusk waiting to be admitted to the museum there were enough places for them to do so.

Holmes walked up and down, surveying the scene, taking in the roadway, the pavement, the windows, the smartly painted doors, the polished gas lamps. Nothing escaped his notice. Nothing seemed to give him any comfort or lighten his dark mood.

I was wondering if Inspector Caldwell might, despite his continued confidence, eventually come to reconsider his conclusion. I said as much to Holmes and he gave a despondent snort.

'Caldwell will never alter his views, and I am not sure I believe in either of his theories. He is most unlikely to spend any more time with the witnesses, something which I think is essential. I have already taken account of the light in this street at the time of the theft, which was adequate for identifying large objects, but I would very much like to speak to the witnesses, since I feel my questions might reveal further information. Unfortunately, I have no authority to do so, and any attempt would only arouse the inspector's fury.'

He walked on a short way up the street still looking about him, and as I stood there wondering whether he would turn back, or if I should follow him, I heard footsteps behind me. The footsteps abruptly increased in pace, and I saw Holmes quickly turn around and stare, then he uttered a sharp cry of alarm. 'Stamford! Look out!'

I spun around, and that one action I believe may have saved my life. The sight I saw then lives on in my memory after all these years, and occasionally wakes me in a nightmare — a man all in dark grey, with such an expression of sheer viciousness on his face, staring eyes and bared stumpy teeth, as I had never before seen on any human being. His arm was raised, and he held a weapon poised to strike. I had no time to avoid it entirely but due to Holmes' warning it did not fall on the back of my head as intended; instead, there was a bolt of pain in my left shoulder, and something hard and heavy glanced on the side of my head knocking me dizzy. Little lights blinked and sparkled before my eyes, and a sudden wave of nausea ran through me.

My legs trembled and I fell to my knees. I was helpless. All I could do was raise my hands in a pathetic attempt to ward off the next blow. But it never fell. As the monster stood over me, raising the weapon once more, Holmes came running up, and ducking expertly under my assailant's guard, delivered a powerful punch to the man's bristly jaw. The cudgel dropped from his hand. It fell to the ground with a clatter and rolled away, and the man, a glazed look in his eyes, clasped both hands to his face, and sat down suddenly on the pavement.

But he had not been alone. Three more men of the same rough type had followed him, and ignoring me and their fallen friend, they advanced on Holmes, cutting off any line of escape. While none of the men was exceptionally tall, all were broad and muscular. Holmes was obliged to back away, but his retreat was abruptly stopped by high spiked railings. The men didn't attack at once but stood before him. All carried clubs and were smacking the bulbous ends into their palms in a threatening manner leaving us in no doubt as to what they were about to do.

'Now then, Mr Holmes,' said one, 'we've got no quarrel with your boy here, who I think has learned his lesson and can run off if he pleases, but you're about to find out what happens to men who go meddling in what doesn't concern them.'

I did my best to cry out for help, and my voice sounded unnaturally shrill and weak. One of the men looked around briefly and I saw him grin. He knew that even if a policeman was to hear me and come running, he would not arrive in time to save Holmes.

Holmes was looking from one to the other and I thought he was calculating how much damage he could do with his fists before he inevitably fell. I tried to stand up, desperate to help him, but my legs would not hold me, and I groaned from the pain in my useless shoulder. Then I saw the club that had been dropped and I managed to crawl over to it. Seizing it gave me some hope. I made a great effort and staggered to my feet. Holmes saw what I was doing and gave a slight nod in my direction. He held his arms up as if in surrender, but I understood what he wanted me to do. I threw the club as hard as I could, grateful for my good cricketing arm and it spun its way true to him. He caught it deftly, plucking it from the air. It was still three against one but at least he was now armed.

And then I saw the true power of the man, the magnificent athlete that could explode without warning from the languid thinker. He started using the club like a cutlass in wide rapid sweeps that caused the roughs to back away. When they came in for the attack, he dealt with them one by one, and the club had become a rapier, parrying and twisting, the skill of his strong wrist sending their weapons flying from their hands until he was the master, he was the danger and not the other way about. It was the most gratifying sight in the world when they all three finally took to their heels.

Their fallen comrade was still groaning on the pavement, holding his jaw as if afraid it might come loose, all his fight gone. He tried to get to his feet and run away but Holmes seized him by one arm and twisted it across his back by some means that made escape impossible, and the miserable fellow squealed in pain. At last, a constable who must have heard the disturbance and my cries, came running up blowing his whistle for assistance. Before long he was joined by another policeman who put my attacker in handcuffs.

Holmes explained that we had been assaulted by four armed robbers, and though the constables looked somewhat doubtful at being told this by a man who appeared to have suffered no more consequences than ruffled hair, there was no denying the four weapons which he handed over, and my injury and confirmation of Holmes' account. Once we had given our statements and names and addresses to the police, the prisoner was taken away.

I had recovered a little by then and on carefully testing the movement of my shoulder established to my relief that the joint was still in place and there were no broken bones.

'And now my dear fellow I must see what a glass of brandy can do for you,' said Holmes. 'My rooms are just around the corner.'

As I had guessed Holmes lived in a modest way, two rooms on the first floor of a lodging house. After assisting me up the stairs, he lit the gas, lowered me gently into an armchair, and furnished the promised brandy. While I sipped this welcome restorative, he placed a match under the coals and we soon had a decent fire in the grate.

I looked about me, and it was something of a surprise that Holmes, who was meticulously neat about his person, was so dreadfully untidy in his surroundings. The small living room at Montague Street was almost impossibly crowded. Its shelves were cluttered with directories and gazetteers which appeared to be in no special order, and there was a large commonplace book stuffed with clippings from newspapers which had not yet been assembled and were spilling from its pages. I saw a few antique volumes bound in cracked leather which he must have purchased from curio shops, some of which were in French and German, and there was a battered old violin in one corner which I remarked upon. Holmes told me that it was a Stradivarius which he was learning to play. Music, as I was later to discover, was one of his great pleasures, although I sometimes wondered if its purpose was to allow his active mind to rest and refresh itself after its labours.

I could not help wondering what Holmes would make of my rooms, where, humble as they are, I like to keep everything just so.

'If you would not object to my looking at the damage,' he said.

'Not at all,' I said, carefully removing my coat, grateful for the thickness of the material that had saved me from worse harm.

'I am sorry to have placed you in danger,' he said, 'and I cannot thank you enough for your prompt action. If you had not been there, I would be a savagely broken man, or a dead one.'

I hardly knew what to say. Holmes bathed the wound on the side of my head and applied a plaster, then having confirmed that my shoulder was merely bruised, he used a scarf to place my arm in a makeshift sling, as gently and carefully as my own dear mother would have done, only without the scolding.

'And now,' he said, 'I have bread and cold meat, and the kitchen will furnish some cocoa so we may make a light supper. And you must rest. The sofa is yours for tonight and I will see you safely to Barts in the morning where I am sure there will be doctors enough to provide a better dressing then I am capable of. I regret I cannot play my violin to soothe you to sleep,' he added, 'since my untrained attempts at a lullaby might keep the neighbourhood awake. Fortunately, the man in the rooms next to these is hard of hearing or my efforts should have drawn complaints before now.'

As we sat before the fire, Holmes revealed that he had been making enquiries to discover how the smoke in the pot had been produced and was working on the chemical analysis of the samples. 'And I may have solved the mystery of Dr Martinson's mysterious light,' he added. He produced a newspaper which carried an advertisement for a pocket lantern, designed to enable persons travelling by night to read in the otherwise pitch darkness of cabs. It carried a modest supply of paraffin and a wick, and it was small and lightweight enough to be suspended from a coat button, while its pierced metal face provided a safe but even glow. 'Not, I suspect, something with which Dr Martinson would have been familiar,' he said, 'although I still have to consider how it appeared to float in mid-air. The injury to your head is of particular interest,' he added. 'Fortunately, it was more in the nature of a glancing blow than a direct strike as suffered by the two attendants, but I am confident that tonight we witnessed the action of similar weapons if not the same ones. These men were not new to their profession. They have used these clubs before. Now Dr

Summerlee in his evidence stated that the injuries to Collier and Finley were similar in form, if in different locations. You observed what was highly significant about the motions of his hands when he pointed them out to the jury?'

'I'm not sure I did.'

'For Collier's injury, he used his left hand. For Finley's, his right. If both men were struck from behind, as seems probable, then Collier's assailant was left-handed and Finley's right-handed.'

'Were any of our attackers left-handed?' In my mind's eye I saw my attacker and had no difficulty in recalling him with his right arm raised against me.

'No. I have fenced left-handed men at college, and I am sure of that.'

'So the murderer is left-handed.'

'It appears so. But I am sure that the inspector with his superior intelligence does not need to be told that.'

'Why do you think Collier said he had felt the blow before he became unconscious?' I asked.

Holmes reflected on this. 'For the present I have no explanation,' he said. 'We only have Robson's word, and he may have misheard or made an assumption.' It was said lightly enough but I could see that Holmes was troubled by the point.

As night descended, we sat in sociable silence, Holmes smoking a clay pipe. I did not smoke; in fact, I abhor the habit and have never taken it up but was content with brandy. My greatcoat served as a coverlet and I was finally able to sleep as long as I made no attempt to move my bruised shoulder.

Next morning after a breakfast of toast and eggs we returned to Barts, where I had an exciting story to tell my fellow students, although taking my cue from Holmes, I made sure to convey the impression that the attack had been an attempt at robbery.

The following afternoon, with my shoulder now dressed in some impressive bandages, I accompanied Holmes to the police court to give our account of the incident. On the way Holmes advised me that he had confirmed that the label on the packing crate was that of taxidermists Ward & Co of 167 Piccadilly. Moreover, his research had revealed that turpentine was used in the art of taxidermy. Our case in that area was complete but we doubted that Inspector Caldwell, who was determined that we were in error, would have listened to us.

The police court proceedings were over quickly. The defendant, his jaw tied up in a cloth like Marley's ghost, was either unwilling or unable to say anything, and was committed for trial at the next assizes. All we learned about him was that his name, which he had been obliged to scrawl on paper, was Joe Rundle, and his stated occupation a labourer at the London Docks.

After recent events I was a little discomfited to see Inspector Caldwell in attendance. I assumed that he had heard about the incident and had come for the personal satisfaction of seeing us at a disadvantage. I was not surprised therefore when he approached us after the hearing.

'I trust you are not in too much agony, Mr Stamford?' he asked, although it was less an expression of sympathy than triumph.

'I am pleased to say that nothing is broken. I am simply bruised.'

'Well, let that be a lesson to you,' he said. 'Choose your friends more carefully in future, and don't meddle in things that are not your concern. As for you, Mr Holmes, I hope this means you will leave criminal matters to the police from now on.'

'I bow to your superior experience,' said Holmes drily.

'Do you now?'

'And I hope to see the stolen property retrieved and the murderer behind bars before long.'

'Well as to the first we continue to follow our leads, as only a large force of properly directed men can do. But I believe that I now know the identity of young Collier's murderer, and with a little more evidence to hand, I hope to be able to charge him soon.'

'Oh, that is good news!' I exclaimed.

'Yes, it seems that he was under our noses all the time. He may even be able to tell us where the stolen item is. Once we jog his memory, that is.'

Holmes stared at the policeman in sudden concern. 'His memory? Am I to understand — surely not — that you suspect Mr Finley?'

Caldwell was surprised at this deduction, but went on, 'As a matter of fact, yes. He has been claiming all this time to have no memory even of entering the workshop, but I have had my doubts about him for a while. No, I thought, what if the story of hearing a noise and going there was simply a ruse, so he could go and unlock the door and let in his criminal associates?'

'Pardon me,' said Holmes, 'but if that was the case, how do you explain his taking Collier with him? Or was he a part of the gang, too?'

'No, we think that Collier just tagged along with him,' said Caldwell. 'We know from Dr Birch that he was eager to learn. But then Finley had to silence him and hit him before he let his friends in, only he hit him a bit too hard, you see. Then he opened the door and handed over his keys.'

'With his right or left hand?' asked Holmes. Caldwell was clearly taken aback by the question. 'And why was Finley attacked?'

'Well, we know they're brutal types, don't we?' said Caldwell, glancing in my direction. 'Maybe they decided that they couldn't trust him to keep quiet and he was better put out of the way. Anyhow we have their friend now and once the doctors can pop his jaw back where it ought to be, we'll see what he has to say.' Caldwell, satisfied with his work, rubbed his hands together and was on his way.

'Well, you are not the only one with theories, Holmes,' I said.

'Theories are cheap, and one must always let the facts drive them,' said Holmes. 'Above all, one must never allow devotion to a theory lead to a temptation to distort or ignore facts. Do you recall the attendant, Robson, saying that Collier had told him Finley had asked him to go with him to investigate a noise? That does not fit Caldwell's theory. But it was pointless for me to mention it. Even if Caldwell was to believe Robson, he could easily brush it aside by saying that Collier had been confused by a blow on the head. At least I have planted the idea of handedness in the inspector's dull brain, and we will see what he will make of it. At present he knows nothing. He has nothing against Finley but is merely casting about for a suspect and has lighted on the nearest man.'

He lowered his chin to his chest, deep in thought. 'Something is wrong in our understanding of this crime; something is very wrong indeed. I only wish I knew what it was.'

CHAPTER SIXTEEN

We made our way back to the museum where we found Dr Martinson at his desk, studying with great intensity through his magnifying glass what appeared to me to be a piece of shapeless rubble, such as might be found lying on any street, but which I realised must be the mysterious Saqqara fragment.

On seeing my heavily bandaged appearance he rose to his feet at once with an expression of alarm. 'Oh dear, Mr Stamford, whatever has happened?' he exclaimed.

'It appears worse than it is,' I said airily. 'Really, it's nothing.'

Martinson looked unconvinced by my attempt at bravado but decided not to press the matter. 'I have heard no news from the inspector, if that is what you have come to ask,' he said, sinking back into his chair with a despondent sigh. 'In the meantime, I am wondering what to do when the museum opens to the public, which it will do in just a few days. The Rosetta Stone is one of our most admired exhibits. People come here on purpose to view it. Scholars study it constantly. We can't simply say that the stone is on loan to another museum because people will ask us where they should go. I have suggested that we put a notice on the plinth to say it has been temporarily removed for cleaning. That is bound to lead to dissatisfaction, but what else can we do? The public will be obliged to accept the absence, but not the gentlemen of the delegation who will be here very soon and will ask to see the cleaning as they will naturally think the stone is in our workshop. Professor Dümichen is coming and Professor Lepsius, they are giants in their field, and I can scarcely lie to such distinguished men. And they are to be joined by Bruno of

Turin and Dubois of Paris. What am I to say to them?' It was obviously a rhetorical question and we had no answers.

'I have come to seek your advice which I think may assist us in locating the stone,' said Holmes. 'To discover its whereabouts, we must start by solving the problem of how it was removed. It has not become invisible, neither has it become as light as air so it might be lifted easily or shrunk so as to be placed in a pocket. Neither, I am sure, has it been broken in pieces, which would undoubtedly have left significant traces. Since the museum's hoist was not used, we don't even know how it was lifted off the plinth. Let us begin with that question.'

'The thieves could have brought their own hoist,' I suggested. 'If they were smart about it and had practised, it might have been done in time.'

'But none of the witnesses saw such a thing being brought,' said Holmes. 'I suppose if it was disassembled it might have lain in the back of the wagon covered by a tarpaulin, and the parts carried in, and reassembled. But if as I believe the thieves had a confederate in the museum, why bring one at all, when there was a serviceable hoist already here?'

'That is true,' I admitted. 'Might they have lifted it off the plinth and onto a barrow by manpower if they had sufficient numbers?'

Holmes turned to Martinson. 'You have told us that the Egyptians when they wished to move large sculptures, items very much larger and heavier than the Rosetta Stone, had their own methods, relying on the power of their great numbers of slaves,' he said. 'Do you think it possible that the stone was lifted from the plinth and then moved by manpower alone? We know that there was a gang of intruders, although not how many of them there were.'

Now that Martinson was engaged in an ancient mystery, he was calmer and more thoughtful. 'I have wondered that myself. But given the weight of the stone it would have required a substantial number of men to do so. Even to lift it from the plinth to place it on something like a sledge would have been a considerable feat of strength.'

He rose and went to his bookshelves, taking out a number of volumes which he brought to his desk and opened. There were numerous drawings of the Rosetta Stone, with detailed descriptions of its markings, which did not assist us, but then after a moment's reflection he opened a drawer in his desk and drew out a copy of *The Illustrated London News*.

'September 1874,' he said, 'the international conference of Orientalists. They visited the museum and were shown the stone by Dr Birch. There is an engraving here which shows the stone as displayed.' He opened the newspaper and laid it on the desk before us, revealing a picture of the Rosetta Stone as we had first seen it, lying in its cradle on the plinth, its surface covered by its protective frame, and surrounded by a group of serious gentlemen, studying the strange language. 'I believe it would have taken the strength of ten men at least to lift it,' said Martinson, 'ten strong men, but given the dimensions and the shape of the stone, ten men could not have safely grasped it. There is no place on the stone itself for a good handhold.'

'What of the cradle the stone rested on?' I asked. 'It is strong enough and has places where it can be grasped.'

'A number of men might have grasped the cradle,' said Martinson, 'but if we look at its structure, we can see that it affords hand grips for far fewer than ten men. It was designed simply to hold the stone tilted for examination, not for transport.'

We examined the illustration and were obliged to agree. 'I really doubt that the thieves would have been able to lift it from the plinth at all, let alone lower it onto a sledge,' said Martinson. 'Any such attempt would have led to failure or even a serious accident. And I have not seen any reports in the news of men suffering crushing injuries or broken backs.'

'And a sledge being pulled along the floor — even supposing they had such a thing — would that not have left marks which would have been seen next morning?' I asked.

'I saw no sign of it,' said Holmes, in a tone which ended any further discussion on that theory. 'I still believe the police are looking in the wrong place,' he went on. 'When we found the wagon at the railways there was a packing crate on it which I now know to have come from the workshop here. If it had nothing to do with the crime it would be the most extraordinary coincidence. But it is pointless to mention this to the police until I have further evidence the inspector cannot brush aside. Dr Martinson, if you could give the question of lifting the stone your expert consideration, I will give the entire conundrum some thought,' said Holmes. 'I sometimes find a quiet session with a pipe or two helps the process.'

Dr Martinson looked alarmed at the prospect of Holmes lighting a match and so with assurances that this would not happen in his presence, we took our leave.

CHAPTER SEVENTEEN

Not far from the museum we found a snug corner of an antiquated hostelry which offered modest and threadbare comfort. Holmes explored his pockets, produced a clay pipe, matches, and a paper bag with a twist of tobacco, settled his long frame in a chair that was far too small for his height, and once the pipe was lit, proceeded to think. My shoulder still ached mightily, and I was grateful to obtain a small medicinal libation to ease my suffering. I knew better than to interrupt his ruminations.

After a long silence, Holmes took the pipe from his mouth and spoke. 'What have been the watchwords throughout this case?' he said, gesturing with the malodorous object. 'Preparation and misdirection. Evidence of the superior controlling mind. A mathematician, you said, and you may well be correct. But every time we find ourselves faced with an obstacle, with some curious feature which we cannot understand, we try to explain it away by chance, or luck or error. But what if we return to first principles and assume instead that not only was everything most carefully prepared and all eventualities were considered in advance, but it also very largely — and I say that because nothing in this world is ever wholly perfect — went to plan.'

Of course, I could do nothing but listen, which I suppose was what Holmes wanted me to do.

'Let us consider the witnesses. There are several people who were in Montague Place that night, each of whom saw a part of the plan being carried out. There is nothing to suppose that they are under suspicion, indeed that is their strength. They are independent, innocent, believable. Did the thieves take steps to avoid being observed? No, they did not. Why was that? The answer is most probably because their actions were not in themselves suspicious, given that the museum was undergoing its usual cleaning. They had no need to conceal what they were doing. Had they tried to do so, that in itself would have made them look suspicious and attracted unwanted attention.' He puffed away at the pipe for another minute or two, and then I saw his expression change, from serious meditation, to a dawning understanding, and finally triumph. 'By Jove, the audacious rascals! I see it now! Of course! One small point and the whole thing becomes as clear as day!'

For a moment I thought he had entirely forgotten my presence and gave a little cough. 'I'm afraid I am still in the dark,' I said.

He laid aside the pipe, which had clearly done its business, leaned forward across the table, and spoke very intently. 'Picture the scene. The witnesses in the street saw three operations; first, the arrival of the wagon, second, the package wrapped in carpets being brought out of the museum on a barrow and lastly, it being lifted onto the wagon by windlass. There are varying accounts of how many men were involved in this endeavour which range from four to seven, but we can assume it was several. Some will have arrived by wagon; others could easily have been lurking nearby. We are unlikely to know their actual numbers.

'Now, there are no reports at all of anyone seeing equipment being carried into the museum. If the thieves had brought their own barrow such an item would have been cumbersome enough to require some time for them to unload. But no one saw it. The noise alone of such an operation might have caused some curtains to twitch. Similarly, with a hoist. Indeed, we have one witness who saw the wagon drawing up and recalls that it had a windlass but did not see any large or unusual items of equipment that it might have had on board.

'Inspector Caldwell has dismissed this witness as unimportant because the account does not match his theory, but I do not. The witness was a schoolboy, and they can often have a prying nature that likes to take notice of things whereas men and women who are assumed to be wiser than schoolboys are often too engrossed in their own affairs to look about them and may notice very little.'

He paused and under his regard it was not too much of an effort to recall my own days as a prying schoolboy.

'I believe you are right, Holmes,' I said, 'but what do you deduce from that?'

'Let us start with the lifting of the stone from the plinth. It was not lifted by the museum hoist, and it appears that the thieves did not bring one. Yet if Dr Martinson is correct, pure manpower alone appears to be impossible.'

'Then how did they do it?'

'How, I do not yet know,' said Holmes, 'but if the Egyptians could do it a thousand or more years ago, I believe modern man should be able to achieve it. The method I have still to determine. But lift it they did.'

That was incontrovertible.

'We also know that neither of the museum's heavy barrows could support the weight of the stone, one because it was not built to do so, and the other because it was damaged, and if our young witness is to be believed the thieves did not bring one. Therefore, it was not carried by either of the museum's barrows or indeed any other. Yet —' he tapped on the table with an index finger, to emphasise his point — 'a loaded barrow was seen leaving the museum. That load was lifted onto the waiting wagon by windlass. I still believe, although I cannot prove it, that the wagon we found is most likely to be the one that was used. But it had a windlass which we now know could not have lifted the weight of the stone. Any attempt to do so would probably have broken the windlass or overturned the wagon.'

'But, if the thieves were as well prepared as you say, why did they hire a wagon that could not bear the weight?' I objected. 'They must have known how much the stone weighed. Unless the men who helped load it were assisting the power of the windlass.'

'One witness said that one or two of the men were aboard the wagon where, I assume, they were operating the windlass and two others were helping to guide the load aboard, which suggests that they were not bearing much of the weight. That was a very astute observation, perhaps more than the thieves had bargained for. And I do not in any case, think that just two men could have given sufficient assistance to help that windlass bear such a load. But you see my point?'

'I'm not sure that I do.'

'I said before that the thieves did not try to avoid being seen by witnesses in Montague Place, because their actions were not in themselves suspicious. But on further consideration I have realised that that is only part of the story. I think that they actually *wanted* to be seen.'

For a few moments I was a little puzzled by this, but then realisation came. 'Oh, I think I understand — you mean it was a part of their plan and was meant to lead the police to look in the wrong place?'

'Ah, you go so far but not far enough,' he said. 'It is really quite simple. Sweep away all the complexities and we arrive at the true plan. Misdirection again.' He leaned back in his chair and smiled. 'Whatever left the museum that night, whatever it was that was carried on a barrow and winched aboard the wagon and taken away, it was not the Rosetta Stone.'

'It wasn't?'

'No.'

'Then what was it?'

'I strongly suspect that it was an empty packing crate wrapped in carpets.'

I took a deep breath. 'Then what you are saying, Holmes, is that the whole exercise with the barrow and the wagon was to make us all believe that that was the way the stone had been removed?'

'Precisely. And as you say, to have everyone including the police, who they must have known would be alerted whatever they said, rushing about looking in all the wrong places. I am sure that Inspector Caldwell is still of the opinion that the stone is aboard a ship and is having his men pursuing and boarding vessels that have departed recently. At least if he is busy with that, he will not cause me any trouble for a while. The entire operation was intended to convince the museum and the police that the stone had been removed to some secret location which would be hard or impossible to find. The result was to strengthen the probability that the very considerable ransom would be paid.'

I resisted the impulse to purchase another drink. I needed a clear mind to assimilate even half of Holmes' theories. 'So the stone is not on a ship?'

'No. It has never been to the docks. I regret the time I wasted there, but one often has to eliminate all the wrong avenues before finding the right one.'

'And it has not been taken away on a train?'

'An item of that weight? I do not see how that is possible without leaving witnesses who will recall it being loaded. And whatever Caldwell says, I feel sure that some discreet enquiries were made along those lines. In any case, it never reached the railway station.'

'Then is it in a warehouse somewhere? But no, I don't see how it was taken there if it wasn't on the wagon. In fact, you have completely baffled me, Holmes. I don't see how any of it happened.'

'You have not followed my reasoning to its final conclusion,' said Holmes, looking amused rather than annoyed at my obtuseness. 'I do not think that the stone has left the museum.'

He allowed me some time to think about it. I stared at him for a while to try and detect any sign that he had concocted some elaborate joke to confuse me. Because I certainly was confused. I waited and watched, expecting to see that he thought I had swallowed his preposterous tale, upon which he would laugh heartily and announce that he had fooled me. But I waited in vain, for he was deadly serious.

'Do you know where it is?' I asked at last.

'Not yet. And I will not know until I can ascertain just how it was transported to its current home. Consider the size of the museum, the many galleries and saloons, the reading room, the stores, the offices, the apartments of the keepers. We have been deluded into believing that the stone has been removed from the building so none of these have been properly searched. They might not have been searched at all.'

'I doubt that Inspector Caldwell would entertain your theory,' I said.

'I am sure that he would not and neither do I believe that even Dr Birch who has been kindness itself, would grant us the permission to make such a search, especially of the private apartments. We have no authority there.'

'What about the attendants?' I said. 'Or the cleaners? If you told Dr Birch what you think, he might direct them to make a search.'

Holmes knocked out the cooled dottle from his pipe into the paper bag, where I realised to my horror that he was saving it for a second smoke, then returned the bag and pipe to his pocket. 'I would prefer not to involve them,' he said, very meaningfully.

'Ah,' I said. 'I believe I understand you.'

'It is a risk we cannot take if we are to get to the heart of the mystery. There is a very good chance that someone working in the museum was in the pay of the thieves. He was perhaps not directly involved in the crime itself but acted as a spy and informant for those who were. How else do you suppose our attackers knew my name? That individual might still be there. We don't know who to trust. Dr Birch told us that the museum has over one hundred employees and I doubt that he was including the servants in the accommodation wings.'

'But it is too large a task for us,' I protested.

'And yet it must be attempted, said Holmes. 'And we must do it soon, before the museum pays the ransom. I will give the question some further thought which will narrow the search, but I must go and see Dr Birch at once before he parts with a penny of public funds.'

CHAPTER EIGHTEEN

We found Dr Birch in his office, looking like a man struggling under a great weight that was resting on his shoulders. He had some papers before him and a pen in his hand, but he did not appear to be doing any actual work.

'Ah, gentlemen,' he said, 'my sympathies. I have just been informed of the dreadful incident last night. What an appalling thing to happen so close to our doors. The police have been here asking questions, but I am afraid no-one could help. That is a very substantial bandage, Mr Stamford. I hope no great damage has been done?'

I made the usual reassuring noises.

'Poor Stamford took the worst of it, I am afraid,' said Holmes, 'but he is a stout fellow and will mend. I have good reason to be grateful to his bravery and cool headedness under attack, or it might have been far worse.'

I tried to look modest. Dr Birch tried not to look surprised.

'It is most distressing. Street thieves are not at all common in this vicinity,' said Birch. 'Public confidence is so very important to us. But I understand that the police have one of the men in custody,' he added. 'That is something at least.'

'They do,' said Holmes, 'but there was no thieving involved. We allowed the police to think that in order to protect the interests of the museum, but it was very clear that the intention was not to rob but to injure — to dissuade me from pursuing my enquiries into the loss of the Rosetta Stone.'

'That is monstrous!' exclaimed Birch, shocked.

'And yet it encourages me to think that I have been on the right track. Had I not been seen as a danger to them, I would not have been worth the trouble.'

Birch seemed little comforted by this. 'I regret that I have heard nothing from Inspector Caldwell regarding the stone, although I understand he is redoubling his efforts and there is a search currently underway of the wharves and warehouses further along the Thames.'

'You have not paid the thieves I hope,' asked Holmes.

'Not yet, but the trustees are working hard to accumulate the necessary funds and will advise me of their results today. I fear that if we are no further forward by tomorrow, we will be obliged to pay something, even if not the full amount. That may placate them for a time. In fact, my greatest hope is they will be content with a smaller sum than their outrageous demand and keep their word by telling us where to find the stone.'

'Before you part with any funds, I must beg a little of your time, as I would like to make a further search in the museum,' said Holmes.

'Oh? Well of course, I am content to allow it. What exactly are you searching for?'

'Any clues, details that may have been previously overlooked,' said Holmes lightly. 'Sometimes the smallest indication can prove vital.'

Birch shrugged wearily. 'Very well. I know Inspector Caldwell has not been happy with your involvement, but he is not here to raise an objection. And last night's attack does suggest that you are making some progress.' He tossed his pen down on his desk. 'I will accompany you in case you have any questions.'

We returned to the museum, and once again found ourselves at our original starting point, the Egyptian gallery. Dr Martinson was there giving some instructions to the cleaners. I saw Holmes stare up at the scaffolding that towered above us, his eyes narrowed in concentration, and wondered if he was thinking if the stone could be concealed there, where it was impossible for us to see it. Then he shook his head and I realised that convenient and ingenious as that solution would have been, such a feat in the available time and with the resources to hand would not have been feasible. The wooden planks lashed to the scaffolding poles were thick and strong and would have borne the weight of several men but would undoubtedly have bowed noticeably or even broken under the concentrated pressure of a slab of stone.

As Holmes looked about him, however, his gaze was suddenly arrested by a carved wall panel, and he went closer to stare at it. It depicted a procession of what I guessed from their scanty and unadorned attire to be slaves. They were proceeding in twos, carrying a litter on their shoulders laden with the form of a dog. It was rather like a hunting dog or pointer with a long snout and sharply erect ears. In view of its size in comparison to the slaves, I guessed that it must be a statue rather than an actual dog.

Had it been in scale, I would not have wanted to encounter such a large beast. I reflected that Egyptian sculptors must have had as little concern for realistic size as they did for so many of the fundamental rules of art. They only ever depicted faces in profile, but the eyes always resolutely and rather alarmingly stared forward. Perhaps they were unable to render them any better on a flat surface, although I note that some of the stranger artists of recent years seem to have made something of a stir doing the same sort of thing quite deliberately.

'Can you tell me what this carving depicts?' asked Holmes.

'Why yes,' said Birch. 'It is a statue of Anubis god of the dead shown in the form of a jackal, being borne by slaves. It was probably part of a funeral procession.'

'Would the statue have been carved from stone?'

'One of that size was most probably painted wood, and gilded.'

'And the structure that it lies upon? What is that called?'

'A palanquin. It is made of wood, and the base on which the statue lies rests on poles. It is a similar principle to the stretcher or the sedan chair.'

'Could such a structure have been used to lift the Rosetta Stone?'

Dr Birch was clearly surprised at this question but gave it some consideration. 'Not a wooden one like this, it would not be strong enough, but the basic principle is sound. It enables the load to be distributed amongst a number of bearers. If constructed of the right materials and with enough men, I suppose something of the sort would serve, but we have nothing of that kind in the museum. I don't think the planks used for scaffolding would do. And how would it be lifted onto them?'

'But there is no need for wooden planks,' said Holmes, going over to inspect the scaffolding, and grasping one of the supporting poles. 'The bed of the Rosetta Stone's palanquin is ready made from iron bars. It is the cradle on which the stone sat. These metal poles, two or possibly four, are equal to the task. And the men were also to hand.'

'I don't understand,' said Dr Birch.

'All it requires is for the poles to be threaded through the bars of the cradle. Perhaps they were lashed to it by ropes for additional security. The men detailed to carry the stone bent to take the weight onto their shoulders and then stood. Strong men, like the brutes who attacked us, dock labourers who handle large heavy loads every day would be able to do it, and it would not take them long.'

Birch stared at the sculpture again. 'I think I see,' he said. 'I know there are doubts about the ability of the barrows to bear the weight, which Caldwell rather brushed aside, but you may have found the answer, at least, to how the stone was lifted off the plinth and carried a short distance. Simple and obvious when it is pointed out. I congratulate you, Mr Holmes.'

'No, rather denounce me as a blind imbecile,' said Holmes, angrily. 'The answer was before my eyes and I failed to see it. Not only that but I did not notice an important clue provided by Dr Martinson at our very first meeting. When he told me about the figures he had sighted and which I believe were dismissed as some visitors who had got lost and were searching for the exit, he said that to him it looked like the funeral procession for a pharaoh. I theorised that what he saw was a rehearsal for the moving of the stone and now I am convinced of it. That done, the men simply pretended to be lost visitors and were conducted out of the museum. All the same, I agree with you on one point; I do not think they can have moved it very far.'

'Then where is it?' asked Birch.

Holmes looked about him. 'The use of the palanquin as opposed to a barrow does not prevent the thieves negotiating a staircase, however they would not have taken it up to the first floor. The distraction of the smoke device in the fossils and mollusc room was designed to draw the attendants away from the seat of their operations. It must have remained on this level. Perhaps we could consider one of the sarcophagi? There is certainly room inside one to conceal it.'

'Hmm,' said Birch. 'That is not an easy thing to accomplish. You may not be aware of it, but a granite lid can weigh several tons, far more than the stone. With time and special equipment, yes, but they had neither.' He looked around him. 'I really don't see any obvious place of concealment in this gallery.'

'I concur,' said Holmes, after some thought. 'We have eliminated one theory as impossible, so let us test another. I will consult with Dr Martinson,' he added, and strode away before either of us could comment.

'He is very — er,' said Birch.

'Unstoppable when he has the bit between his teeth?' I ventured.

Birch grunted. 'I am not sure that was the exact expression I had in mind.'

Holmes had a brief conference with Martinson, and together they walked along the gallery with Martinson pointing out the location of his sighting and also the direction of travel.

Holmes returned to us, accompanied by Martinson, making us a party of four. 'Let us walk,' said Holmes. I had expected him to lead us to the front steps of the museum, but he did not, pausing instead at the door to the basement.

'That door is always kept locked unless someone needs to go in there, but that is not often,' said Birch. 'Would the thieves have been able to enter? The door has not been forced.'

'I have a confession to make,' said Martinson, shamefacedly. 'I had quite forgotten that as well as the outer door keys Finley also had a basement key in his possession.'

'Then we must certainly go in,' said Holmes.

'I regret it will be rather gloomy,' said Birch, calling over an attendant and asking for the new senior man to bring his set of keys.

'With your permission I shall throw some light onto it,' said Holmes. He reached into his pocket and took out a small metal box which I recognised as the new lantern he had shown me pictured in an advertisement. 'I bring you the compact pocket lantern,' he said. 'A boon to the gentleman traveller at night who wishes to read his newspaper. It may be suspended from a coat button by the handle, leaving both hands free. I have no doubt, Dr Martinson, that a device of this kind provided the light you saw, the glow passing through the metal mesh of the casing, the lantern appearing to float in the air as it was carried suspended from a pole.'

It was rather an expensive acquisition for a medical student, but I had seen that Holmes lived in a very abstemious way, and I wondered if the little lamp had cost him a number of dinners.

'Well,' said Dr Birch, examining the lantern, 'as you know, lights of any kind are forbidden in the museum.' He spent a few moments considering how to proceed. 'These are special circumstances. Martinson, would you approve?'

Dr Martinson, who had stared at the pocket lantern with nervous dread took a deep trembling breath. 'Mr Holmes, it would be a terrible thing if it were to be dropped. There are a number of things in the basement which are flammable and should not be endangered.'

'I could bring a fire bucket,' I said. 'That would be more than enough to deal with any accident.' The museum was well provided with sand buckets, and I fetched the nearest one.

Martinson and Birch stared at each other. 'I believe that we must do what is necessary,' said Martinson. Birch agreed.

The keys arrived and Dr Birch unlocked the door. 'Before we go in,' said Holmes, 'do you know when this door was last unlocked?'

'I do,' said Martinson. 'I unlocked it myself only a few days ago when I showed you around the museum. You recall how dim the light was then, since we only have a little sunlight coming though the upper gratings at certain hours.'

'And no-one has been down there since?'

'Not to my knowledge.'

'Excellent. Then let us descend.'

CHAPTER NINETEEN

As the door opened, Holmes struck a match, ignited the wick in his pocket lantern, closed the front and suspended the device from his coat. The glow passing through the perforated cover cast a pale diffused blush over the walls. Before us was a set of stone steps leading down, with a simple wooden handrail, worn by years of use, as the only assurance of a safe descent. I recalled being told that the basement was part of the old Montague House that had once been the museum's home on the same site. It must originally have been a repository for wines and other comestibles.

Holmes began to make his way slowly down the steps, taking great care and looking about him as he went. We followed cautiously. As we negotiated the darkened stairwell, I estimated that if the thieves had descended this way carrying the stone between poles the passage was wide enough for their purpose. At the bottom of the steps, however, there was a sharp turn leading to another flight, which I thought might have caused them some difficulty. Here Holmes stopped and looked around with particular attention. Then he made a sudden exclamation and pointed to something on the wall.

'What is it, Holmes?' I asked.

'See there!' He shone the lantern for us and indicated a distinct scratch on the rough whitewashed stone. 'It looks fresh, too. I don't think it was there before. If I am not mistaken it was caused by contact with the end of one of the scaffolding poles as the men turned the corner and confirms my theory.'

At the bottom of the stairs, we reached a low-ceilinged storeroom, in which the only available light was from a small grating. It was crowded with artefacts from times long past and many places. They were in good order but not displayed in a manner for easy viewing. In the public part of the museum, the larger exhibits were necessarily surrounded by space for visitors to pass, with smaller items protected under glass. This was not the case in the underground store. The eerie light of the lantern revealed the shapes of sculptures ranged closely along the walls, their eyeless faces regarding us with the impassive wisdom of the ages. There were mummy cases, furniture, pottery, carvings in wood and ominous shapes bound in grey linen. The floor was packed with boxes in each of which dozens of objects, wrapped and labelled, nestled in straw.

I find it hard to describe the odour of that place of antiquities. The smell, whatever it was, made me think of sand and ancient dust and desert, with a sweet exotic hint of incense. It was like entering a forgotten tomb and smelling air that had not been breathed in thousands of years. We walked slowly through the place, with Holmes all the time casting the lantern's glow like a filmy veil over the stored treasures but finding nothing of any great size. I saw no items or boxes that could not have been carried down the stairs by two men sharing the load. Taking great care not to tilt the lantern, Holmes bent down and perused the surface of the floor with his magnifying glass, looking keenly at the patterns of footsteps in the dust. He was like a bloodhound on the scent, looking everywhere, with every sense engaged.

'What are you looking for?' asked Dr Birch.

'Footprints,' said Holmes. 'I do not believe this floor is swept as often as that of the galleries, for which I must be grateful.

There are older ones here, those of booted feet, the kind of boots worn by your attendants, but you recall the marks that were made in blood in the workshop, which revealed that the feet of robbers were encased in soft soles. Well, I see some of those here, and they are on top of the boot prints.' There was nothing else of importance to be found in that room, and he followed the trail which moved through the space and led us to a second room.

This next room was lined with banks of deep wooden shelves, which were crowded with smaller unwrapped items. Some of the shelves stored materials used for the upkeep of the building, such as tools, brushes and paint, as well as baskets and trays, ropes and straw packaging. Others were filled with exhibits of every kind, statuettes, vessels, fragments of sculptures, carved figures, scroll cases, tiles and plaques. Not all was Egyptian — I saw broken pieces of classical figures, torsos, limbs, fallen heads with hair like ripples in marble. Once again, I inhaled the intoxicating fragrance of the ages.

'There has been a great deal of activity here,' said Holmes, studying the floor. 'See how the dust has been agitated by many feet. But now, yes — here are the soft soled shoes again, sliding along, slowly, deliberately, as if the men are carrying something very weighty. They lead us here.' He crouched down to the floor then peered underneath the lowest shelf where there was a tumble of small crates. 'We need to move some of these pieces out, look where there are drag marks on the floor. And these markings — unusual, but I think I can guess what they signify!'

I did my best to assist with my one good arm, and both Birch and Martinson moved some of the boxes aside. Holmes got to his knees and shone the lantern underneath.

There was a long expectant pause. 'What do you see, Holmes!' I asked at last.

'Nothing as yet, but I think that a sheet of wood, the inner lid of an old crate, has been put here vertically and wedged into place. I think it is hiding something.' And so he began his exploration, like an Egyptologist negotiating a narrow crumbling passageway in an ancient tomb.

Holmes, despite his height, managed to fold his long thin frame like an acrobat and held the lantern before his eyes, taking care to maintain it upright. The shelf above him was constructed of planks and there was enough space between them for the rest of us to see a little of his progress. He crawled forward by inches, then there was the sound of wood scraping across stone, and at last, with an exclamation of triumph he had the obstruction free. A dusty piece of wood was pushed out from under the shelf towards us.

'Holmes?' asked Birch.

After a moment or two, Holmes, his hair sticking up in spikes and covered in dust, crawled back out to greet us. He coughed and thumped his chest with a fist to clear his throat, then gave us a broad smile. 'Take a look, gentlemen,' he said.

Birch and Martinson both knelt down as swiftly as they were able, and I gingerly lowered myself to the floor, while Holmes shone his lantern under the shelf for us. There, pushed to the back against the wall was the Rosetta Stone, complete with its iron cradle and glass protective case. It was resting on a number of the shorter length scaffolding poles.

'The ancients could not have done better,' said Holmes. 'The criminals have used the old technique of sliding a large weight on rollers to push it right to the back of the space. The marks left in the dust left me in no doubt of that. Since the poles are still there, extraction will not be hard. I think the longer poles used to carry the stone have been replaced to where they were taken from and we will find if we examine them that one has a fresh scraping of whitewash at one end.'

There were several seconds of silence, and I wondered at this before I realised that Dr Birch was speechless with emotion, while Martinson, after a great deal of effort, managed to half stifle a sob. Both the older men sank to the floor and sat there in an undignified manner which would have astonished their associates.

'It is a miracle!' said Birch at last. 'Mr Holmes, I don't know what to say — I don't know how to thank you.'

'I truly cannot express how grateful we are!' said Martinson.

'No thanks are necessary,' said Holmes. 'It was just a matter of logic. I am pleased to have been of service.'

'I must take a closer look,' said Martinson, anxiously. 'I need to see if there has been any damage.'

'I will hold the lantern for you,' said Holmes.

Martinson was still very nervous of the little light but was grateful that someone else had charge of it. He crawled carefully under the shelf, accompanied by Holmes with the light.

Dr Birch climbed to his feet. I saw him put out a hand and lean for one moment against the edge of one of the upper shelves. After that moment of weakness, he straightened up. 'Well, Martinson?' he asked.

'No, wonder of wonders it appears to be quite intact,' said Martinson, with a little gasp of relief. 'The glass case too.'

'We need to examine it in better light,' said Birch. 'If nothing else it will need thorough cleaning.'

Martinson emerged from under the shelf. 'I will supervise all the arrangements personally,' he said. 'If all is well, I really do think we will be able to see it back in its rightful place for the opening.'

Holmes has risen to his feet and was calmly dusting down the knees of his trousers. Both Martinson and Birch, who were now beaming in relief, clapped him on the shoulders and explained in rather disjointed terms words to the effect that he was a splendid fellow, adding many expressions of eternal gratitude.

'I will summon our attendants,' said Birch, 'and we will have it removed and taken to the workshop. I assume it will be possible to bring it up in much the same manner as it came down.'

'If I might make a suggestion,' said Holmes, languidly.

Birch and Martinson paused and stared at him. I was struck by the fact that though they were his seniors in every respect and would not usually have unquestioningly taken the advice of a youthful student, their expressions told me that they were looking to him for guidance. As well they might, as he had proved himself by finding the stone, but it was more than that. To any person of discernment, Holmes displayed an air of assurance that almost commanded others to listen to him and follow his advice. Only those who were so content in their own ability that they thought themselves always superior to others, such as Inspector Caldwell, were unable or unwilling to recognise this.

'At this moment it would be best if as few persons as possible knew that the stone has been found,' said Holmes. 'I feel sure that the criminal gang has placed one of their spies in the museum, a spy who might well still be employed here. I do not, of course, suspect either of you gentlemen.' Dr Birch and Dr Martinson both treated this comment as a moment of dry humour before they abruptly realised that Holmes was perfectly serious. 'As it so happens,' Holmes went on, 'I have an alibi for the abstraction of the stone as I was working in the chemistry laboratory at the time. There are a number of extremely irritated gentlemen at Barts who can attest to that. And I am happy to vouch for Mr Stamford. This means that at present no member of the criminal gang, including its controlling genius, is yet aware of our discovery. You should also consider that when the museum re-opens to the public, members of the gang will be free to enter as visitors and see for themselves whether or not the stone has been restored.'

'That is true,' said Birch, cautiously, 'but what do you suggest we do?'

'I advise that the stone should not be placed on public display. In fact, it should remain exactly where it is for now. We must replace everything exactly as we found it. The finding of the stone must be kept secret to everyone outside this room, apart of course from the police. My reasoning is this. If the gang see that the stone has been found, they will know that no ransom can be expected. They may decide to abandon the scheme, in which case they will not be caught. If on the other hand they believe they can still get their money, you may receive another communication from them which will furnish us with a valuable clue and enable the police to apprehend them. There is, after all, a murderer at large.'

'I agree,' said Birch, reluctantly.

'But what will I tell the delegation?' said Martinson. 'They arrive tomorrow.'

'You have a day to decide,' said Holmes. 'But do not be tempted to tell them of the theft or so much as hint at where the stone is. People talk.'

CHAPTER TWENTY

'And now it only remains to give Inspector Caldwell the good news, since he is currently employing considerable police resources looking in all the wrong places,' said Holmes.

'Ah yes,' said Dr Birch. 'I shall take on that duty. An urgent telegram to the police station. I expect it will bring him running here. I cannot fault him for energy at least.'

'You should also suggest to him,' said Holmes, who was clearly enjoying his moment of triumph, 'that the wagon which Stamford and I located is not to be dismissed from his consideration after all, but should, as I originally stated, be treated as a part of the criminals' master plan. It was an elaborate ruse to divert enquiries away from the museum premises. Further enquiries might provide some clues. The packing case found on board, the purpose of which was to make us think the stone was being removed, was taken from the museum, probably from the workshop. The recent purchase of sunbirds from Ward & Co was delivered in it. If you have a spy here, he may well have placed it in readiness for his friends to use.'

'Do you suspect anyone in particular?' asked Birch, as we climbed the stairs up to the ground floor.

'Not yet, but based on the inquest evidence I believe it is possible that whoever struck poor Collier was left-handed. There was only a small number of attendants in the museum that night. It might have been one of them.'

'I will do my best to look into that,' said Birch.

We returned to Dr Birch's apartments where he despatched his servant with a telegram form, and provided us with a celebratory glass of sherry, although Dr Martinson said he would be content with water.

'I am only sorry that because of the necessary secrecy the museum did not offer a reward for the stone's recovery,' said Birch, 'but I will ask the trustees to arrange a suitable gift for you both. I know how hard the student years can be.' We murmured our appreciation of the gesture, but really, I don't think either of us was expecting a reward.

As the congratulations flew and Holmes made some slight attempt at modesty which quickly evaporated under the torrent of praise, I also detected a shadow of concern in his manner. Much as it pleased him to discover the stone, I could see that the loss of a man's life, a youth of his own years, weighed heavily upon his mind, and I thought how hard it might be to lay that crime at someone's door.

The servant returned from his errand. 'Dr Birch, Mrs Finley is at the door and begs to be allowed to see you. She is in a state of great distress.'

'Poor woman,' said Birch, 'yes, please admit her, I will see her of course. I fear bad news of her husband.'

We waited in more sombre mood than before, and Holmes, having despatched his sherry, declined another and paced silently and thoughtfully about the room.

Mrs Finley was a respectable looking lady of about forty, plainly attired, but showing every sign of recent neglect of her appearance by the careless disorder of her hair and the strain apparent in her features.

'Dr Birch!' she exclaimed then her lips trembled, and she was unable to restrain tears and began searching about her person distractedly for a handkerchief. Dr Birch was obliged to lend her one of his own, while Martinson led her to a chair and saw her comfortably seated, then brought her a glass of water.

'I am so sorry to intrude on you gentlemen and in such a state, but I had nowhere to turn,' she said.

'It is no intrusion I assure you,' said Birch kindly. 'Please let us know what we can do for you. You may speak freely before Dr Martinson and also my associates Holmes and Stamford.'

'It's Harold,' she said, 'my poor husband. The police have been questioning him about what happened at the museum. I don't know the whole of it, but I have been told there was another attendant who was attacked and has died of his injuries. Harold has been very bad, but he is more himself now, though he can't remember anything of what happened. This morning the police came again and asked if he could come to the station to answer some more questions, and he went with them gladly, saying he would do anything he could to help them.' She broke off into fresh sobs but quickly made a brave attempt to control her grief so she could go on with her story. 'Not an hour ago a policeman came and told me that Harold had been charged with murder. He is locked in the cells now. I went to see him, and there was a police surgeon there who has examined him and says he is well enough to be charged, although he advised it should be left a few more days before he goes before the magistrates. Harold is as well as can be expected but very despondent as you can imagine. He still can't remember being attacked however hard he tries. He thinks there must be an hour or more that has just gone from his mind. There's an inspector who keeps saying that Harold is just pretending but I know he is not. Even the surgeon says that he has seen this kind of thing before after a blow to the head, but he can't say if the memory will ever come back. But even if it does, even if Harold remembers it all and knows he is innocent, I don't know if he would be believed, there's no witness to what went on. Dr Birch, I've no one to turn to!'

Dr Birch drew up a chair before the anguished woman and took her hands gently in his. 'Mrs Finley, I have known your husband for many years, ever since he came to work here and there has never been any question of his honesty or integrity. I will appeal to the trustees on your behalf to grant him any assistance he may require. If it is necessary, I shall provide testimony as to his good character.'

She thanked him through fresh tears. 'I need to get something to take for his dinner,' she said. 'I don't know what they feed them in that place.'

'Come with me,' said Birch, 'my wife will be able to provide something.' The unhappy woman leaned on his arm and he conducted her from the office.

'I had feared this,' said Holmes. 'Even without evidence the inspector presses ahead and manufactures a conclusion. We must do what we can before any further damage is done.'

Martinson could only look helpless.

Dr Birch returned with a determined expression. 'And now,' he said solemnly, 'I have some letters to write. And I am sure to receive a visit from Inspector Caldwell before long. Mr Holmes, I hope you don't mind but it would be best if —'

'I agree — I shall not confront the inspector,' said Holmes.

'I expect he will want to look in the storeroom,' said Martinson, 'and I know he will insist on using one of those big lanterns. Oh dear!'

'I will conduct him and ensure that all is done in safety,' said Birch. 'Martinson, I suggest you continue your preparations for the delegation.'

Martinson hurried away, looking somewhat relieved.

'Even with a police lantern, I doubt that Inspector Caldwell will see any more than you were able to,' said Birch.

'I am sorry to say,' said Holmes, 'that Inspector Caldwell sees the world as a horse does through blinkers. He has a narrow view which is modelled on his past experiences but sheltered from anything requiring use of his imagination. No doubt this serves him well for the everyday and commonplace, but it can be a hindrance when faced with a crime such as this one.'

We took our leave of Dr Birch and as we walked towards Great Russell Street, we narrowly missed encountering Inspector Caldwell as he hurried up, rather red in the face, puffing hard with the effort, Sergeant Lestrade striding along behind him.

A new thought occurred to me. 'What of the man who has been charged with assaulting us?' I asked Holmes. 'He and the others might have been part of the gang that moved the stone that night. He might even know who struck Collier and Finley. Surely the inspector will be able to draw the truth from him.'

Holmes did not share my confidence. 'That rogue is merely a cog in the system. Paid generously by coin for his work and told to question nothing. I doubt he even knows or cares who his real master is. And if he does know anything, even if he witnessed the murder, even if offered clemency for his own crimes in return for his evidence, he will not speak. He knows what his fate will be if he does. Retribution will find him, even in prison.'

'I suppose there is nothing more you can do now,' I said.

'Far from it,' said Holmes. 'The criminals did leave us with one very important clue, one which the inspector considers not to be of any importance now that he has men in custody. I doubt that he is pursuing it, but I fully intend to.'

CHAPTER TWENTY-ONE

I did not see much of Holmes in the next two days. The many tasks and distractions of our enquiries meant that I had fallen well behind in my studies and it was necessary to apply myself diligently to my work. Fortunately, I do not have the antipathy to hard work which I have noticed in so many of my fellow students. I have often wondered if that was the quality Watson saw in me which led him to suggest I study surgery; not any great innate intelligence but the ability to devote myself wholeheartedly to my labours, although perhaps I ought to mention with just a touch of humble pride, the extraordinary neatness of my bandages.

I knew from reports that Holmes was spending long hours in the chemistry laboratory, both on the experiments required by his course and some private work of his own, which often meant he stayed on for many hours long after the other students had left to pursue more convivial activities. I even heard a rumour that he had almost set the laboratory on fire on more than one occasion, but I always thought that those incidents were greatly exaggerated by those who did not know him. Holmes was adventurous and eager to experiment in his pursuit of the unknown, but not careless. Of course, word had got about in Barts that I was a crony of his and some of the students and even one or two of the lecturers sought me out to ask what I thought Holmes was doing. Fortunately, I was able to reply in all honesty that I didn't know as he had told me nothing. And then, shortly afterwards, as he was so often wont to do, he vanished, none of us knew where.

I heard nothing more from the police and could only wait to be called as a witness when my brute of an attacker appeared for his trial. How I wished I could have been present to see the expression on Inspector Caldwell's face when he learned from Dr Birch that after all his efforts at the docks the Rosetta Stone had been found in the very last place he had thought to look.

I had been studying the newspapers for any reports relating to the museum, and saw that it had re-opened to the public, its time of closure for the day advanced by an hour to allow for the brighter spring weather. I was then better placed with my studies and the pain in my shoulder was considerably reduced, the injury no longer requiring me to support my arm in a sling, although the bruising was all the colours of the rainbow. I therefore decided on a refreshing stroll to Bloomsbury.

The museum was crowded with visitors eager to make the best of the clear unclouded light pouring through the freshly scoured windows. The plinth of the Rosetta Stone was still empty, but a card had been placed on it to inform the public that the exhibit had been temporarily removed for cleaning. Even so, there were visitors ringed around it, standing two or three deep, as if mere proximity to the plinth was something to savour. I looked at their faces and listened to their conversation, wondering if I was in the presence of one of the criminals, but they looked respectable enough. Most were silent, and only a few speculated on when the stone might return.

I saw Dr Martinson nearby, occupied with a small group who were discussing the inscription on a sculpture with every evidence that they could actually understand it. I wondered if this was the anxiously awaited delegation of Egyptian experts, although he had mentioned four names to me, and the group consisted of three gentlemen and a lady. I guessed that one of the scholars must be travelling with his wife or sister. I decided not to interrupt their academic discussion. Martinson, however, chanced to see me and while I made a polite nod of greeting in his direction, he excused himself for a moment and came to speak to me.

He enquired after my injured shoulder and I was able to reassure him that I was mending well and congratulated him on the good order of the museum. He was still eager to have the stone restored to its proper place but felt obliged to follow Holmes' advice on the matter. 'The public are naturally disappointed,' he said. 'I have been advising them that we hope to have it back for viewing next week. The delegates will still be in London then, as they are visiting other museums and they have promised to return to see it. So far I do not think anyone entertains a suspicion of what has really occurred.'

'Has anything more been heard from the thieves?' I asked.

He shook his head miserably.

'As a matter of curiosity,' I said, 'how will the stone be brought back up the stairs? It will be a hard thing to do if it is not to take any damage.'

'That is something of a challenge, but we will follow Mr Holmes' theory of how it came to be there in the first place. We mean to use ropes to draw it across the poles until it is out from under the shelf, but then we will construct a makeshift palanquin, lashing it to longer poles which will enable a team of attendants to carry it. It will need the brawn of quite a number of strong men.' He looked almost misty-eyed. 'It will be like enacting something from ancient times.'

I thought that the procedure would make an interesting sight and said I wished I could be there to see it. 'I assume that Inspector Caldwell has been fully apprised of events?'

Martinson's face was immediately covered by a wintry cloud. 'Oh, I am very glad that Mr Holmes was not there to reveal his triumph. It did not go well. Obviously, the inspector was very pleased that the stone had been found, as it has saved him and his men a great deal of effort, although the circumstances of the discovery has prevented him from claiming any credit for it. In fact, he was downright suspicious at first, and levelled all kinds of contemptible accusations against the museum and Mr Holmes as well.'

'I don't understand,' I said.

'Would you believe, he actually turned round and accused us of playing some sort of game or trick in order to gain publicity to increase visitors so that we can get a bigger grant from Parliament? He said that in all crimes of this nature one has to see where the money goes, and whoever gains is the criminal. I pointed out to him that this was a serious matter what with the death of poor Collier and did he really imagine the museum had arranged that? He was obliged to admit that he did not but thought that Collier's death was only because something had gone wrong with the plan, and that was the real reason why the disappearance of the stone had to be kept secret. Otherwise, it would have been all over the newspapers in a trice.'

'How did he think Holmes was involved?'

'He didn't say, only muttered that he had his suspicions. I doubt there was any foundation for them. But he clearly disapproves of Holmes and will look for any opportunity to censure him.'

'Is he going to take this further?' I asked, alarmed at this development.

'Oh no, he dares not. Dr Birch was quite disgusted with him and told him in no uncertain terms that any accusations of that nature if made public would reach the trustees of the museum and might be taken before Parliament. In fact, Dr Birch made it plain that he would be perfectly satisfied if it did go before Parliament as the museum had nothing to hide, but he doubted that Inspector Caldwell would feel the same way. At that, the inspector finally saw sense and closed his mouth. Is Mr Holmes about?' he added.

I was obliged to inform him that Holmes was busy with his studies although I thought that he was also pursuing some enquiries on behalf of the museum. 'I expect that Caldwell, too, for all his faults is also still at work on the case.'

'Do you think so?' asked Martinson, dubiously. 'I'm not so sure. As far as Caldwell is concerned, he is a busy man with many other cases to pursue, and he might consider both the theft and the murder to be solved crimes. He has two men in custody, and he thinks all he has to do is get them to confess.'

'Is there any news of Finley?'

'Poor Finley has been brought before the magistrates, but he was still unwell, and the hearing has been adjourned. I don't think Caldwell has enough evidence for the case to go to trial. But if the charges against Finley are dropped and he is released then the accusation will hang over him like a curse unless the crime can be solved.'

The little group he had been conducting about the museum had moved on, and the delegates were now within earshot of our conversation. All discussion on the theft and murder necessarily ceased.

'We have been engaged in a further examination of the Saqqara fragment,' said Martinson, 'and it has been such a boon to have so many expert minds on the problem. We also have the benefit of some additional pieces from the same site, and there are exhibits we already hold from the fifth dynasty for comparison. Sadly, there may be no more material to be recovered from that tomb, since I have been advised that it has recently been declared unsafe to enter. Attempts to shore up the roof have only made it worse, and I fear we may lose it entirely.'

The visitors joined us, and it was necessary for Martinson to introduce me as one of Dr Birch's junior assistants. They were an interesting assembly of persons and I decided to try and apply Holmes' methods and observe them very carefully to see what I could deduce. Professor Johannes Dümichen of Strasbourg was a gentleman who I judged to be not especially aged but with an extraordinarily high domed hairless skull which, so I have been told, often signifies huge intelligence, and the longest beard I have ever seen, which signifies I know not what. It did lend him a mature erudite air, which might have been the intention. I was informed that he was the very man who, while working in Abydos in 1864, had discovered the famed list of Pharaohs, the drawing of which I had earlier seen in Martinson's study. He was German by birth and greeted me politely in heavily accented English. By contrast Professor Karl Lepsius of Berlin, although appearing rather older than Dümichen, had been gifted with a flowing mane of pure white hair and a noble moustache of the same hue, so he resembled an elderly lion. He was apparently extremely famous for having produced an illustrated work on the antiquities of Egypt in twelve large volumes, which was, so I was assured, essential reading. He, like Dümichen, had German as his native tongue but spoke good English.

The third gentleman was a Dr Antonio Bruno of the University of Turin, which enjoyed an unrivalled collection of Egyptian antiquities. The great Champollion, I was told, had studied its papyri when decoding the inscriptions on the Rosetta Stone. Bruno was a rather nondescript fellow of about thirty-five, with dark hair cropped in tufts and a thin moustache. He had almost nothing to say for himself, and I gathered that he spoke very little English. The lady was a Madame Dubois of Paris. She was aged about forty, with a dignified yet mild expression. Unlike the other lady visitors who I think came not only to see but be seen, she was dressed in a very plain and modest style, a black gown with neat white collar and cuffs, no jewellery of any kind, and an old-fashioned bonnet, with no trimmings. She wore spectacles and carried a notebook and pencil. I was surprised when I greeted her to find that she spoke the most perfect English. It transpired that Dr Bruno, while having little command of our language, did speak tolerable French. Whenever anything was communicated in English therefore, Madame Dubois repeated it to him in French upon which he responded in that tongue and smiled and gestured and nodded a great deal to the rest of us, to show that he understood.

When asked about my own studies I did my best to deflect any close questioning by admitting a very humble status, thus preventing my exposure as a complete ignoramus on the subject of ancient Egypt.

As I returned to Barts I reflected on the fact that both Holmes and the delegation were in their own quite different ways addressing themselves to mysteries, and mused for a while on the constant search of the human mind for truth.

CHAPTER TWENTY-TWO

When I next entered the chemistry laboratory, I understood why so many of the students were concerned about Holmes' work. There was a peculiar odour and a dangerous looking grey haze in the air. Holmes, serenely unperturbed, was giving all his attention to the contents of a row of beakers, which appeared mainly to consist of ashes. There were pieces of what looked like charred pasteboard and burnt cord scattered carelessly on the bench.

'You have been causing some alarm,' I said, gently.

'Progress can be alarming to many,' he observed unrepentantly.

'But I think I can guess what you are working on.' I glanced about me, but the only other student present had adopted a pained expression and decided to abandon his work and retire from the scene. 'The clue you mentioned — the smoke device?' I asked, when we were finally alone.

'Indeed. You recall that I took a sample of the ash from the clay pot and noting what the attendants said about the material's behaviour once ignited and their unsuccessful efforts to extinguish it, I have spent some time working on its composition and trying to build a smoke maker of my own. If one knows what one is doing, then it is a simple enough matter. However, I do not believe that the hirelings who were engaged simply for their bodily strength would have known how to make one.'

'You spoke of a superior intelligence behind the scheme. I suppose he would know.'

'Yes, a man who is the master of all, but without ever risking himself or dirtying his hands. He does no more than devise the plans, for profit, of course, but principally, I think, for amusement, to bolster his sense of superiority. Such a man would employ able lieutenants to manage his exploits and hire and command his troops. I believe that there must be a member of his retinue who has both the knowledge and the easy access to the materials to build the item.'

'Have you succeeded?'

'Oh, yes, several times, but only in miniature. For some reason my modest endeavours to test the effectiveness have met with disapproval and were reported to the warden, who expressed some strong opinions on the subject. But now I have another test to carry out and it had better be done in the open air and far from the knowledge of Inspector Caldwell, who would like nothing better than an excuse to arrest me.'

'Dear me, Holmes, what are you about to do?'

'I have constructed a smoke device of the right dimensions and I mean to set light to it. Therefore, I must take a trip into the countryside to some remote spot where my experiment may take place without danger of discovery. Hyde Park and Hampstead Heath have too many police patrols for comfort.'

'But there will be danger to yourself, Holmes,' I said. 'You should not go alone.'

'Thank you for your concern, Stamford. If you would be willing to accompany me and act as witness, we could take a sandwich and bottled beer and make a picnic of it.'

I wasn't sure if he was joking or not but naturally, I agreed.

Holmes still had some final adjustments to make, and we appointed to meet close by St Paul's early the following morning. He arrived true to the chosen hour, carrying a well-laden knapsack the weight of which did nothing to slow his energetic stride as we walked up to the railway station.

'I have had one small disappointment today,' said Holmes. 'I received a note from Dr Birch. You recall that I advised him of my belief that Collier's assailant was left-handed. He has been very careful in his enquiries and observations so as not to alert anyone, but he has now established that none of the attendants in the museum on the night of the attack was left-handed. The murderer must therefore have been a member of the gang of hired brutes, and we may never be certain of rounding them all up.'

It was not hard for us to find the open and less frequently patrolled spaces Holmes needed for his experiment. London in those days had more green fields and country lanes than it does now. Locations which today are familiar to us as crowded with narrow streets and the habitations of thousands were then farmland and common pasture. Hard as it might be to imagine, in 1876, the thoroughfare of Portobello Road, or Lane as it was then called, was regarded as a pleasant rural walk. It needed only a short train ride from Liverpool Street to reach the cornfields that lay north of Notting Hill.

As we travelled, I told Holmes about my recent visit to the museum, the conversation with Dr Martinson and my observation of the appearance and behaviour of the delegates. He questioned me closely, paying especial attention to the size and shape of Professor Dümichen's head and the style of Madame Dubois' bonnet.

We alighted at small rural station and proceeded to complete our journey on foot. The weather was dry and of that perfect mildness which is not too warm for walking, the air fresh and invigorating, scented with greenery. We passed some small dwellings, where simple but well-tended gardens were planted with vegetables and flowers. While I could not help but be uplifted by the bustle of London, I found the peace and calm of the countryside a delightful contrast and could not help but comment on the beauty of nature and the appeal of the simple life.

'And yet,' said Holmes, solemnly, 'the very isolation of these scattered homesteads brings dangers of its own. Just think what terrible crimes might be carried out in such places in the certain knowledge that no help is at hand for the victim? Only a few years ago in just such a humble cottage as we are passing now, an entire family of seven were bludgeoned to death and no-one heard their screams.'

I have to say this grim statement did rather dampen my enthusiasm for the countryside.

After a mile or two we left the lane and walked up a footpath between some fields. Finding a sheltered spot between hedgerows where there was a passing space for farm carts we stopped at last and laid clean kerchiefs on the ground to sit on.

Holmes opened his knapsack and produced two bottles of beer and a paper of beef sandwiches. My contribution to the feast was a fruit cake, a gift from my mother who was convinced that since I was a student I never had enough to eat. Holmes then brought out a simple pottery vessel and placed it on the earth before us. Inside rested his experimental device which he lifted out for my inspection with a smile of satisfaction. 'As you see, from its size it would not be advisable to test it indoors, or it might cause some alarm. I believe however that it is perfectly safe.'

The exterior was a piece of supple card or thick paper which had been formed into a hollow tube and secured with adhesive, the base composed of the same material. It was filled with a light-coloured granular substance the nature of which I could not determine. Some strands of thick black cord protruded from the interior and these were connected to a longer cord which was wound around the casing.

As Holmes described his recent work, we delved into our picnic, and with appetites stimulated by our walk, made short work of it. Had it not been for the incendiary object in front of me, it would have been a perfectly pleasurable outing.

'I have spent many hours analysing the burnt material in the clay pot left in the museum,' said Holmes. 'The difficulty was that it was composed of a number of different things and was mostly in the form of ash. There was the blackened remnant of a sulphur match, and with careful sifting I detected some small flakes of what appeared to be compressed card which would have been a good container. The material inside it is a mixture of saltpetre, sugar and wax. I am not sure if I have the proportions exactly right, but I feel I am not far from it.

'There must also have been something to provide ignition of the mixture — I have used ordinary string which I soaked and coated in a little black powder. If the man who lit it had any sense of his own safety, there would also have been a longer, slower burning fuse. I deduce rather than detect its presence. Bickford fuse is a common enough type.

'Fuses alone when lit will produce some smoke but not nearly enough for the thieves' requirements. What they wanted to achieve was a substantial distraction. The mixture in the tube will produce a fair quantity of smoke but no flame. Once lit, and a simple sulphur match will suffice, the safety fuse will give the perpetrator enough time to retreat. There may be a few sparks but that is all, and in any case, they will be contained within the clay pot.

'Once the material ignites it will start to produce smoke. Initially, the museum attendants tried to put it out by pouring on sand from a fire bucket and then inverting the bucket over the pot, thus cutting off the supply of air. That might quench an ordinary fire but in this case the mixture has its own supply of oxygen from the saltpetre, so that did not work. Then they threw water on it, which might have cooled it, but again that was probably insufficient to extinguish it. My experiments have convinced me that once started this material will tend to burn until it is almost wholly consumed. Now then, shall we begin?'

I have to say that by this time I was extremely nervous, but all I could do was nod and hope that all would go well. Holmes set the clay pot on a patch of dry earth, and I retreated to a distance where I felt at the very least safe from immediate combustion.

Holmes struck a match and lit the end of the fuse. He rose and moved back, but not as far as I had gone, his eyes fixed on the process of his experiment. The cord was consumed slowly, the blackened burnt trail climbing up inexorably towards the faster fuse. Certainly, there was more than enough time for the person who applied the match to retreat an appreciable distance from the scene. The short fuse with its coating of black powder ignited with a brief hiss, and I saw a little fiery glow. Before long, a wisp of smoke began to pour from the pot, gradually increasing as the reaction took hold until dense grey clouds rose and swelled, far exceeding the size of the vessel, rather like a genie of the old tales pouring like mist from a magic lamp.

Holmes gave a great laugh of triumph. 'There, it does exactly what I anticipated, and we have only to imagine what that must have looked like when found unexpectedly in the confines of the fossils and mollusc saloon. The whole room must have been filled with a dense blinding smoke. I must admire the courage of the men who faced it and tried to tackle it.'

'The alarm and the noise would have ensured that the gang had more than enough time to move the stone,' I said, 'and they would not have been heard.'

The smoke was just beginning to die down when we heard a shout from along the footpath and saw advancing towards us at a run, a thickset fellow of middle years, in country clothes and gaiters, bright red in the face, waving a long staff, and demanding to know what we were doing.

'I believe that may be the farmer. Time we were gone,' said Holmes, calmly, as he knocked the ash from the pot and thrust it and the remains of our picnic into his knapsack. 'Come, Stamford, I think we can out-run him!'

We took to our heels and bounded back along the footpath like a pair of mischievous schoolboys. Holmes seemed to have not a care in the world, although I confess that as I ran, I was less in fear of the farmer's ire than I was of any repercussions from our adventure that would endanger my academic career and distress my parents. Our pursuer, however, by reason of greater age and dimensions was soon out of breath, and at length his shouts faded into the distance, and we reached the lane and were able to return to the station, our reputations intact.

CHAPTER TWENTY-THREE

I was somewhat alarmed the following day to receive an unexpected visit at Barts from Sergeant Lestrade; in fact, I was quite prepared to be arrested on the basis of the angry farmer's complaint. I hope I didn't look too guilty. To my relief Lestrade's first question was, 'You wouldn't have seen Holmes about?'

'He's hard to track down sometimes,' I said, still feeling a little cautious, but trying to be helpful in case it benefitted me in front of the magistrates, 'but I can think of some places where he might be found. Come with me.'

Lestrade merely nodded without revealing the reason for his enquiry and trotted along beside me as we looked for his quarry. He was an odd looking fellow, some ten or twelve years my senior, with a sharp pugnacious face, always with brows pulled down in concentration, giving him the expression of a worried gun dog. I had the impression that he would, like a dog, once he had seen his target, follow it for as long as it took, and then fasten his teeth in and not let go. There might not have been a lot of imagination in the man but there was certainly a great deal of energy and a will to do what was right.

I decided not to ask him any questions, as I felt he might not be forthcoming, and in any case, I wasn't certain I wanted to know the answers. After a brief search we found Holmes in the dissection room, preparing some slides for the microscope. It was a meticulous and delicate process, requiring great care and concentration, and I would certainly not have wished to interrupt anyone undertaking it.

'Mr Holmes, might I trouble you?' asked Lestrade.

'Fire away,' said Holmes, casually, continuing to work.

Lestrade shuffled his feet a little. 'I just wanted to say first of all, that the police force appreciates all you did in finding the Rosetta Stone. It saved us a lot of man-hours. I mean, we would have got to it eventually I am sure.'

'Once you had searched every ship and warehouse at the docks,' said Holmes in amusement.

'Well, yes, there is that. And who knows we might still find out something there to help us. The man who attacked you gentlemen we know to have been a dock hand, and his friends are probably the same. But I thought I ought to come by and say what needs to be said, as I don't think Inspector Caldwell would. Especially as he had hoped to get the kudos himself, and now it is all yours to claim.'

'I claim nothing,' said Holmes, airily. 'Caldwell may have the glory if he wishes, it means nothing to me. After all, what would I do with it? I suspect that the whole affair will never appear in the press.'

'Ah, well, no,' said Lestrade. 'It's a sensitive business, what with the annual grant to the museum yet to be decided. Dr Birch is very anxious about that.'

'Are you any nearer to arresting the rest of the gang?' asked Holmes.

The sergeant's morose expression was answer enough. 'We were hoping that the men we already have in custody would be the best way to identify them, but Finley still says he has no memory of the crime and denies having any part in it. The inspector continues to question him, hoping to break him down, but all he says is he remembers coming to himself lying on the floor, with Collier near him. Then he heard Robson calling out and trying to rouse them both. Nothing more. And the other fellow, well he has closed his mouth like an oyster out of fear. Whatever frights him is worse than a dozen Caldwells.' Lestrade shuffled his feet again. 'I don't suppose you have any other observations, Mr Holmes?' he added.

Holmes took some time to lay out his work neatly. He had reached the stage where it only remained for the rim of adhesive around the thin glass covers which protected his samples to be left to dry, but I doubted that Lestrade would have known that. There was something very deliberate in Holmes' movements and I sensed that he was rather enjoying keeping the sergeant in suspense. 'Tell me, has the inspector directed any attention to the smoke device planted in the museum?' he said at last.

'Ah, yes, but without result so far. He thought it might have been something employed by conjurors, and we have been making enquiries with that in mind, but no-one admits to having used or made, bought or supplied such a thing. In fact, when we asked conjurors about it, they said they don't like to use real fire, they have chemical tricks to make little puffs of colour — it's not real smoke at all. Also, the theatres are too afraid of fire, and the appearance of anything that looks like real smoke on the stage might cause a panic in the audience, and people could be trampled to death in the rush for the exit.'

'I have established that the material in the body of the device was a mixture of sugar, wax and saltpetre,' said Holmes. 'Saltpetre is used both for pickling meat and the manufacture of gunpowder. There must also have been something to ignite the material and a safety fuse to delay ignition, but no trace of those remains and I can only speculate on what they might have been, although I doubt that they were anything out of the common way of such things. The crucial ingredient however, which is less common, is the knowledge of how such a device is to be made.'

'Well, any butcher or grocer and not a few cooks or housewives will know how to pickle meat,' said Lestrade, 'but a smoke maker of that sort is another thing. I don't think Mrs Beeton covered that in her book. And there are no gunpowder mills in London, for which I am very grateful. An accident in a gunpowder mill is never a trivial thing, and I wouldn't want to deal with one.'

At this, a curious expression passed over Holmes' face and he gave the sergeant his close attention. 'Do you know where the nearest one is?' he asked.

'Somewhere in Essex, I think. Mr Holmes, if you were to find out anything that would help the police, I am sure you would let us know.'

'I will let *you* know, Sergeant,' said Holmes. It was obvious from his emphasis that he had no intention of communicating with Inspector Caldwell.

'One other thing, Mr Holmes,' said Lestrade, 'I — er — I did hear say that Dr Martinson saw some — well, I suppose they might be called ghosts in the museum after dark? Is that right? Or is it just a story?'

'I can reassure you that there was nothing ghostly about what Dr Martinson saw,' said Holmes. 'Just thieves in the dark.'

Lestrade puffed out his cheeks in relief. 'That's good because I would rather tackle a whole gang of desperate men than one of those spirit things.'

Lestrade thanked us and departed, after which Holmes was silent and thoughtful for a time. Then he examined the slides, labelled them and arranged them carefully in a box marked with his initials, which he set to one side. 'I am done here for the day,' he said.

'You look as if you have a trail to follow,' I said.

'I do. It may be nothing, it may be something. But it must be followed, and I do not think Lestrade, for all his determination, is the man for the task.'

I had no need to ask whom he believed the right man to be.

CHAPTER TWENTY-FOUR

Two more days passed during which I heard nothing from Holmes, and I was able to buckle down to my studies. He did not appear at Barts, even in the students' reading room, and neither did I receive a visit from Lestrade or Caldwell.

When I heard from Holmes again it took the form of a curt note saying that he was to meet with Dr Birch and Dr Martinson at the museum in an hour and would welcome my attendance if at all possible. I had completed some of my work a little ahead of time anticipating just such a possibility and was able to comply.

We gathered in Dr Birch's office, and I saw at once that there were serious faces all around me. I wondered what Holmes had been doing since I had last seen him. I suppose I had imagined him following footprints along a path somewhere with his magnifying glass, his long nose pressed near to the ground, and making little cries of delight at his findings. Such an activity he appeared to find refreshing rather than tiring, but that day he looked strained and weary.

'There has been another letter from the criminals,' said Birch. 'It arrived in today's post. Mr Holmes, I know you wished to see it before it is passed to the police, and of course now that we have the stone, I am less concerned than I was about a short delay.'

He handed Holmes an envelope. Holmes carefully studied both sides of the envelope, then extracted its contents, a single sheet of paper, which he read, looked at the reverse side, and held up to the light. He then laid the envelope and the letter on the desk and subjected them both to a minute examination with his lens.

'What does it say?' I asked.

'It reads, "To Dr Birch, you are warned that the full amount must be paid as directed by next Monday or the museum will lose it most prized possession forever. No further warning will be given",' said Holmes.

'Clearly they do not know that it has been found,' said Birch. 'Your advice on that matter was sound.'

'Dr Birch,' said Holmes, 'I do not believe the police will allow me to see the first note, and I am therefore hoping that you are able to recall as many details of it as you can in order that I might compare it with this one. The paper, the ink, a mark, a stain, anything at all would be of use.'

'I did examine the first one to see if it might tell me anything,' said Birch, 'but it was a common type of ivory wove notepaper, the sort that might be had at any stationer's, at three sheets and an envelope for a halfpenny.'

'You mentioned before that the paper was clean, but the envelope was dirty,' said Holmes.

Birch gave this some thought. 'Yes, the envelope was a little smeared with dirt, from fingers I think, but the paper inside was clean.'

'And you told us that the words were inked over several times to disguise the hand?'

'Yes.'

'Do you think it resembled the writing on this note?'

'It is hard to judge without the two side by side, but I would venture to say that this is a more educated style.'

Holmes digested this sparse information. 'Here we have paper and envelope both clean, moderate weight, cream laid, better quality than the first. The hand is bold and masculine, but elegant. It too has been inked over more than once, with a good firm nib. We must conclude that this is the work of a different person from the one who wrote the first note. The first note was simply left in place by one of the persons who lifted the stone from the plinth, although I would suspect from the cleanliness of the contents that this was not the person who wrote it. This one, however has been posted to ensure that it reaches Dr Birch, and also because the author does not wish to suggest that it originates from anyone in the museum.'

'Do you know who wrote it?' asked Birch.

'Not yet, however I believe I do know who wrote the first one and also the identity of one of his confederates.'

We were all quite astounded by this simple statement.

'Really?' exclaimed Birch.

'I am about to reveal the results of my recent enquiries,' said Holmes, casually. 'You will wish to inform the police and I suggest that the man to advise is Sergeant Lestrade who appears to be more amenable to common sense than the inspector.' He looked around at us, but no-one dissented. 'As you will recall shortly after the abstraction of the stone, I came to the conclusion that Henry Collier was a member of the criminal gang, and might have been feigning injury, but almost immediately afterwards we were told that he had died, and I therefore abandoned that idea. I now realise that I was premature in doing so. I recently analysed a sample from the smoke device that was ignited in the museum and detected the presence of saltpetre, which is used amongst other things in the manufacture of gunpowder. I recalled also that Collier's family lived in the vicinity of Epping. When I attended the inquest on Collier, I saw that his father had an old injury to his face and was missing an eye. At the time, I guessed that he might be of farming stock and what I saw was the result of a not uncommon accident, the explosion of his own gun. It was clearly some sort of powder injury. But once I had made enquiries and found that there is a royal gunpowder mill at Waltham Cross not far from Epping, I considered that there might be another explanation.

'It was not hard to discover more. I went up to Epping in disguise as a labouring man. I obtained some journeyman work at the powder mill, made some new acquaintances, and visited some of the public houses there. A willingness to work hard, followed by beer and tobacco soon loosened a few tongues. I learned that Collier's father and brother are both employed at the powder mill and Collier was, too, before he came to London. I heard tell that young Henry always felt he was too good for labouring or indeed, any work at all, and had ambitions to live by his wits. He had been dismissed from the mill because there were suspicions of stealing which could not be proven. But he had the knowledge to make a simple smoke device and since he often visited his family, access to all the materials he needed.

'In London he worked as a porter in the London Regent Hotel. Such places are from time to time the targets of thieves who wish to make away with the jewels of important residents. I think it must have been there that he was initiated into a gang who thought they could make use of his quick wits and knowledge of gunpowder. Last year there was a robbery at the hotel. The contents of the safe were taken during an alarm concerning a fire in the kitchens, the origins of which were never discovered. Collier was not suspected of involvement.'

'I don't understand,' said Dr Birch. 'Why was Collier killed? If what you say is true, he would have been a valuable and trusted member of the gang.'

'Indeed, he was. His task was to report a suspicious noise to lure Finley into the workshop where he was struck down so the keys could be taken. Collier then let in his confederates who had been lurking outside and they waited until the time came to play their part.'

'Are you saying it was Collier who struck Finley?' exclaimed Birch.

'I believe so. He was not a large man, but he had worked in a powder mill where, as I have good reason to know, some robustness is required.' At this Holmes carefully rotated his shoulders as if easing an ache. 'He was quite strong enough for what he had to do. Collier then had the task for which he alone was competent, placing the pot with the smoke device and igniting it, then giving the alarm. I imagine the pot had been prepared in advance and concealed in the workroom. An old clay pot is not a remarkable object to see in a museum. You recall that there was a smear of blood on its base. I think it was Finley's, one of the spots and smears on the floor transferring to Collier's fingers as he searched for the keys.

'Once he had given the alarm, Collier had to return to the workshop. His confederates could now proceed to carry out the crime and put the ransom letter in place while the other attendants were busy dealing with the supposed fire. Collier had most probably written the letter under the direction of a senior gang member. But in order to appear an innocent victim Collier had to receive an injury. One of his confederates was therefore asked to deliver a light blow to Collier's head, just enough to produce a bruise, so he could claim to have been knocked unconscious, and then tie him up. Unfortunately, as we now know, there was a weakness in the skull which had never been previously suspected.'

'Do you know who that individual was?'

'I have my suspicions. But before we proceed, I must urge you, if we are to have any chance of discovering more, no-one outside this room other than the police must know that the stone has been found.'

Naturally we all agreed.

'And now I wish you to think carefully,' he said. 'Have you noticed anyone in the museum, either staff or visitors, behaving in a manner that has aroused your suspicions? I ask because I remain convinced that at least one member of the gang is still here, and others may be entering with the usual visitors and perhaps showing more than the expected interest in the absence of the stone?'

'I have not noticed anything,' said Birch.

Martinson shook his head. 'The visitors all ask the usual questions, but nothing out of the ordinary.'

'And the attendants?'

'They go about their work as usual.'

'And what of the members of the delegation? Have you met them all before?'

To my surprise Martinson looked positively shaken by the question. His jaw dropped in amazement, his lips trembled, and he was unable to make a coherent response.

'I hope you don't suspect any of them,' said Dr Birch, with a short laugh. 'All are extremely well known in their field. The gentlemen have published several books and numerous papers. Madame Dubois has assisted at many excavations, and is noted for the excellence of her drawings, which illustrated both her late husband's and her brother's work.'

Holmes said nothing to this, but merely nodded in acceptance. From our previous conversations I thought I knew what he was thinking, of the intelligent minds that lay behind great crimes, and the fact that such individuals had the means and skill to conceal their villainy from the world. He baulked at pointing this out to Dr Birch, who clearly thought that academic excellence precluded dishonesty.

'Have you anything to say to me, Dr Martinson?' he asked.

'I — why, no, no, I can only agree with what Dr Birch has said,' replied Martinson quickly, but he was quite obviously flustered.

'And now, Dr Birch,' said Holmes, 'I have two more questions to ask. Have any of the attendants in the museum recently been asked to work longer hours than usual or take on additional duties, in order to increase their wages? Or are they to be offered a bonus?'

'Why, no,' said Birch.

'In that case I would like you to summon Mr Robson as I have some questions for him.'

'Very well,' said Birch. 'Of course, Robson is in the clear,' he added. 'He and the other attendants who were there that night are all right-handed.'

'Robson was extremely upset at Collier's death,' added Martinson.

'I have no doubt of that,' said Holmes, confidently. 'None at all.'

'You recall of course that it happened in his home,' said Birch. 'Mrs Robson was terribly upset also.'

'Yes,' said Holmes, 'I spoke to her yesterday when I took a look at the room for rent. They have twin boys and three little girls as well. Not the most peaceful household. I was obliged to decline as it was not conducive for study. But we did have a very interesting conversation.'

'What do you think Robson can tell us that he has not already?' said Martinson.

'A very great deal,' said Holmes.

CHAPTER TWENTY-FIVE

While we waited for Robson, Dr Birch sat down to write a letter to the police and dispatched his servant to deliver it. Soon afterwards Robson arrived, and looked at us with an expression of concern. He was a little puffy and bruised about the eyes, which suggested sleepless nights, and he wearily and gratefully took the proffered chair.

'Now then, Robson,' said Birch, gently, 'Mr Holmes here would like to ask you a few questions. Please do your best to answer them.'

Holmes sat facing the attendant. His posture was casual, his air of command inescapable. 'The fact is, Robson,' said Holmes, conversationally, 'that you know a great deal more about the night the stone was taken than you have been telling us. We are now aware of the part that Collier played in its abstraction, and we believe that he drew you into the scheme. That is true, isn't it?'

Robson, jaded and exhausted, gave a great gulp, and looked for a moment as if he would protest, but such was Holmes' calm certainty that he capitulated. 'It wasn't what you think — I didn't mean —' he began, then his lips trembled, and tears started in his eyes.

'Go on,' said Holmes, relentlessly.

Robson passed the back of one hand across his eyes. I saw Birch glance quickly at Martinson, and suddenly realised why. Robson had used his right hand. 'He said it was just a joke,' said Robson, 'a kind of prank. We wouldn't actually steal anything, so it wasn't really a crime. The stone wouldn't be taken away, it would just be hidden somewhere. He didn't tell me where, but it wouldn't be harmed, and whoever had care of it would see it was kept safe. Collier said he was going to see to that part of it, as he knew some people who could do it. And then when it was seen to be missing, the museum was bound to offer a handsome reward for finding it. So he would say he had found it and claim the reward, and if I helped out, we could share it. I mean, it didn't sound bad. And I needed the money. Two more mouths to feed. I wasn't sure if I should do it at first, I mean I didn't know for sure if there would be a reward, but Collier was so certain there would be that he advanced me money on it. And after that, well, I had to go on with it.'

'Of course, you needed to explain the extra money to your wife, so you told her you were being paid a bonus for extra duties,' said Holmes.

'How do you know?'

'Never mind that. Now then, Robson, you must realise that you are in a lot of trouble, and I suggest you make things easier for yourself by telling us all the truth. What part did you play in the scheme? What did you do that night?'

Robson took a deep breath of sheer misery, but I felt that he was preparing himself to lighten his load of guilt. 'Collier said he was going to set off a little firework — it was just something that would make smoke, nothing that would harm anything. I was worried about that, but he said he had used them before, and knew them to be safe. Once he had lit it and given the alarm, I had to make sure to guide the other men to find it so they could put it out. If they wanted to call out the fire brigade, I had to say something like, "it's all right, it's just smoke, not fire", but I think they saw that for themselves. Collier was going to steal the keys from Finley's pocket and let his friends in to move the stone. But he didn't want to be suspected, so then I had to come and tie him up and pretend to have found him like that.'

'Who struck Finley?' demanded Holmes.

Robson gave a little sob. 'You must believe me! I didn't know that was going to happen. I thought when Collier talked about stealing Finley's keys, he meant he was just going to pick his pocket. So when I walked in to the workshop and found Finley lying on the floor, all tied up and blood on his head —' Robson caught his breath and needed some moments to recover and go on speaking. 'I knew that Collier must have done it. And he was calm as anything about it. Then Collier said — he said I had to make it look like he had been attacked too. He had some sort of a stick. He said I had to tap him on the head, just enough to leave a bruise. I swear that was all I did. But he asked me to do it.'

'You are right-handed,' said Holmes. 'Up to this point I had assumed that Collier's assailant was left-handed, because a criminal would have come up behind him to strike. But of course, as his confederate you would have been facing him when you did it.'

'It was nothing,' Robson protested, 'nothing at all. He was conscious and he said it hardly hurt. Then I had to tie him up, and put a gag in his mouth, and put the stick down by his side, because he said his friends would come and take it away. After that I had to leave him and come back later and find them. Collier told me what I had to say. But you have to believe me, I didn't mean any harm to anyone! Collier wasn't much hurt, and we took him home, and the doctor came and said he would just need rest, and we looked after him the best we could, but — I don't know what happened. I didn't think he would die. I never meant him to die.'

'Did you write the letter that was left for Dr Birch that night?' asked Holmes.

'No, I don't know anything about that. I did see Collier with an envelope in his pocket earlier on, but he didn't have it when I tied him up.'

'We've received another letter. It came by post today. What do you know about that?'

Robson's expression of bewilderment told us all we needed to know. 'Nothing,' he said. 'But there was one thing — it happened yesterday.'

Holmes leaned forward intently with his chin resting on the back of his hands.

'It was getting late, and I was helping to usher visitors out as usual, and there were only a few left and it was dark, and then I heard this voice behind me.'

'What sort of a voice?'

'It was hard to tell. I think whoever it was must have been speaking through a handkerchief or a newspaper or a book and whispering. I couldn't even tell if it was a man or woman.'

'What did this voice say?'

'It said "don't turn around". I was afraid. I did glance about a little, just right and left with my eyes, but there was no-one nearby and I dared not call out, I thought I might be killed. Then the voice said, "where is Collier?" and I said, "he's dead". And there was a bit of a pause, then, "has it been found?" Of course, I knew what was meant, and I said, "no, it hasn't". Then everything went very quiet and all I heard were footsteps moving away, and after a bit I did dare turn round to look but no-one was there.'

'Did you get any impression of an accent?' asked Holmes. 'Was the speaker a foreigner?'

'I — no, I don't think so.'

'One more question,' said Holmes. 'We now know that both Collier and you were in the pay of the thieves who took the stone. If there are any others you know of, especially if they are employed in the museum, you must tell us their names now.'

'I swear we were the only ones,' said Robson. Holmes gave him a hard look, but after a moment appeared to be satisfied with the answer.

Robson hung his head and subsided into wretchedness.

Dr Birch strode forward and looked down on the museum's once trusted employee with a thunderous expression. 'I am appalled,' he said. 'Whatever excuses you present, whatever you say to try and make light of your role in this horrible business, I am left with a great sense of betrayal. How can I be expected to believe a word you say? In vain do you claim you wished only to benefit your family. Your criminal actions, your foolishness have now ensured that your wife and five children will lose their means of support. There will be prison for you, and penury for them.'

'Oh, the poor innocents!' exclaimed Martinson. 'I will see if there are any charities who might be able to assist them.'

At that moment the servant arrived bringing Sergeant Lestrade. Both stared in astonishment at Robson who was now openly weeping.

Holmes rose to his feet and delivered the ransom letter to the policeman. 'This has arrived today, and I place it in your hands to be delivered to Inspector Caldwell. You may need to summon the assistance of a constable to take Mr Robson into custody, since I have just received his confession of his part in the recent attempt to defraud the museum and the murder of Mr Collier.'

Robson wailed loudly and blurted out something unintelligible.

'I hope and trust,' Holmes went on, 'that we will very soon learn that Mr Finley who is entirely innocent has been released and all charges against him withdrawn.'

'I don't know what to say!' exclaimed Lestrade. 'I wish we had you on the police force Mr Holmes. Have you ever thought of joining?'

'Never,' said Holmes.

Robson managed to catch his breath and pressed a handkerchief to his eyes. 'I'll come quietly,' he said. 'I won't be any trouble, I promise. I'll make a full statement. Tell you everything I know. Finley had nothing to do with it.' He blew his nose loudly. 'Can someone go and tell my wife?'

'I'll see it done,' said Birch.

Robson rose to his feet and held out his hands to be cuffed.

'If you don't mind, Sergeant, I will arrange for a cab to take you both to the station,' said Birch. 'And I must ask you to be as discreet as possible. Perhaps forgo the handcuffs on this occasion? I don't want the public to see a uniformed attendant under arrest.'

Lestrade agreed, and before long he had departed with his remorseful prisoner.

'Well, you have astounded us again, Mr Holmes,' said Birch. 'I am so pleased that Finley has been exonerated. He is a good man.'

'And now may we restore the stone to its rightful place?' asked Martinson, eagerly.

Holmes was thoughtful. 'If you would be willing to keep its discovery and location secret for just a little longer, there is another task to be carried out. Robson said that he had received a message from an unknown person, someone who I am guessing is a senior individual in the gang, and clearly not a person who works here but who has been admitted to the museum since it re-opened. I have some thoughts on the matter, but I will say nothing about them at present. That person had two spies in the museum, Collier, who must have been the man who reported directly to him, and Robson. But with Collier dead, and Robson now under arrest, his sources of information have just been cut off. We have the upper hand. If we can identify and apprehend this person, we will be closer to the man who masterminded the enterprise.'

'But how do you propose to do that?' asked Birch.

'I have a scheme in mind, but I will need your co-operation,' said Holmes, 'and you too, Dr Martinson, and Stamford, too. Is it agreed?' He looked at us all. We could do nothing but agree and wonder at what would happen next.

CHAPTER TWENTY-SIX

The following day Holmes and I made our way to the museum for a meeting with Dr Birch, Dr Martinson and the members of the expert delegation. 'You will be amused to know,' said Holmes, 'that in order for my plan to succeed, Dr Birch has represented me to his distinguished visitors to be something of a prodigy in the preservation of ancient artefacts. My interest in chemistry might prove useful in that deception. The ruse is designed to lend me some authority but also to avoid my being examined by the delegates on areas of history which do not form any part of my studies.'

'What is the purpose of your studies, Holmes?' I asked impulsively. 'Do you intend to teach?'

He smiled. 'I am expanding my mind to enable me to instruct and enlighten the ignorant, and bring them to a better understanding,' he said. I had the impression that that was the best answer I would receive. 'You have, I assume, deduced that Madame Dubois is the lady who many years ago was betrothed to Dr Martinson,' he added.

'I — er — no, but now you say it —'

'The likelihood was very strong from the start. Their first meeting in Egypt when assisting her brother on an excavation, which is something we know Madame Dubois to have done, and the adoption of the style of bonnet which characterises her as a member of the Society of Friends.'

I realised then of course, that the reason the lady spoke such perfect English was that she was an Englishwoman. I must say I felt rather foolish. 'And you are certain of it now?'

'Yes, it has been confirmed by the lady herself. I received an unexpected visit from Madame Dubois yesterday,' said Holmes.

I was too astonished to comment.

'Shortly after arriving in London, Madame Dubois had a private interview with Dr Martinson. She told him how gratified she is that he is now one of the Society and hoped that they might be better acquainted in future, if only in a professional capacity. She suggested that they might like to correspond with a view to collaboration on some fields of research. To her great surprise Dr Martinson revealed to her that the admiration and esteem he had felt for her all those years ago was unchanged — in fact he became quite emotional on the subject. He did not however believe that any closer association would be appropriate as he did not feel he was worthy of her. More than that he would not say. Madame Dubois is both a perceptive and determined lady. She approached Dr Birch to enquire if her old acquaintance had some terrible trouble on his mind, but he was unable to enlighten her. He did, however, comment that if she sought someone who was able to solve unusual mysteries than she might consider consulting me.'

'Your fame is spreading, Holmes,' I said. I am not sure he was pleased or otherwise at this thought.

'She came to see me at Barts.' He paused. 'I do not anticipate any comments from the other students concerning our interview. Nothing scandalous can be concluded from a visit by a lady of her years and such modest appearance and demeanour. Nevertheless, if anyone was to ask, you might inform them that the lady is an aunt of mine.'

I could see that Holmes was a little embarrassed by the prospect of undeserved notoriety and promised to do as he asked. 'Were you able to advise her?' I asked.

'Not yet,' he said. 'But she has given me some further information to consider, and as a result I find that some of my previous assumptions based on first impressions were incorrect. It was not unreasonable to suppose that Dr Martinson became a member of the Society of Friends and adopted the way of temperance soon after his betrothed, who was then a Miss Stephens, asked to be released from their engagement on the grounds of his excessive fondness for alcohol. I had thought his decision was made in order to win her back. I have now learned that this was not the case.

'Initially Dr Martinson had not been especially religious, but he did attend some meetings of the Society when he and Miss Stephens decided they wished to marry. She had hoped he would be accepted into the Society before they married, but he could not renounce his old habits and they parted. Several months later, Miss Stephens was working on some drawings for one of her brother's publications when she was introduced to a Dr Dubois of Paris, and they were married soon afterwards. She occasionally heard from mutual acquaintances that Martinson had been very deeply affected when he learnt of her marriage and had spent long periods of time unwell and distracted. She had no difficulty in understanding what was meant by those words. Then a year or so later, she was told of his heroism in trying to save the lives of his sister and brother-in-law in that tragic fire. It appears that this was the event which produced his new fervour for religion.'

'I have heard of people undergoing such a conversion when they have looked death in the face,' I said.

'Indeed, and given his great regard for the lady it is not surprising that he turned for support and comfort to the Society of which she is a member and an example,' said Holmes.

'He still loves her,' I said. 'But does she still love him?'

'A lady may dissemble in many things,' said Holmes, 'but I do not think she can produce artificially the colour that rises to her cheeks when she speaks of the man she loves and wishes to marry. The question that mystifies her is the reason why he still considers himself unworthy of her regard. He has done all he can to redeem himself. He is in every way a good husband for her. One might have imagined that a repenting sinner is someone who would excite sympathy rather than disgust.'

'Once he had abjured liquor everything in his life appears to be blameless, exemplary,' I said. 'His bravery, his scholarship, his devotion to his orphaned nephew.'

'Yes,' said Holmes, thoughtfully. 'George Luckhurst said that his uncle had become a second father to him. I fear, I greatly fear that there may be another truth, one which is buried deeper than any ancient tomb, and which may never see the light of day.'

CHAPTER TWENTY-SEVEN

Soon afterwards we arrived in Dr Birch's study, where he, Martinson and the delegates were seated around his desk. Substantial as this surface was, all irrelevant materials had been set aside, and a space had been cleared for a tray on which in cushioned splendour lay the precious Saqqara fragment and the additional pieces brought by the delegates. There were hand lenses available for all, as well as more powerful ones mounted on brass stands, and everyone had brought notepaper and writing materials. The curtains of the study had been drawn back and secured by cords. It was a bright and sunny morning, with all the advantages of natural light over the artificial and often misleading glow of gas lamps.

Mme Dubois had doffed her dark and serious bonnet and her hair was gathered underneath a plain starched white cap which framed her face in a way that was both attractive and modest. Dr Martinson, who was also in his usual black with a white collar, matched her well. It was almost as if they were the models for a pair of mantelpiece ornaments. I thought it would be a great shame if they could not be reunited at least in friendship, however, the bearing of them both at the meeting was formal and dignified.

'Thank you, madame and gentlemen,' said Dr Birch. 'I am hoping that by gathering together we may be able to contribute further thoughts on these precious fragments, now that we have all had the opportunity of making a study of them together. My assistants are here to learn and also to take the notes of our meeting. We are greatly indebted to Madame Dubois who has been kind enough to bring to our attention the pieces discovered by her brother and which have now been proven as coming from the unidentified tomb. I trust that we are all agreed?'

'Most certainly,' said Martinson, 'the location of the discovery and certain appearances on the surface of the rock leave me in no doubt. And I believe that there may be some part of the original carving still remaining —' he leaned forward with the tip of a pencil as a pointer — 'here, and here.' The delegates leaned forward to make their examinations.

'But just before we begin,' said Birch, 'there is something of importance I wish to share with you. We are away from observation of the public and I think that as a courtesy I should make it known to you, in case you were ever to hear idle rumours, the truth of the events which have taken place in the museum very recently, and the real reason why the Rosetta Stone is not currently on display.'

As I had been instructed, I looked very carefully at the faces of the four delegates. Three of them raised their heads to gaze at Dr Birch, and were all attention, but Bruno still bore the same fixed smile, and was still addressing himself to the fragments. Madame Dubois whispered to him briefly in French and he looked startled and sat up.

'I will hand you over to my assistant, Mr Holmes, who has been working with us on this matter,' said Birch.

'As you have seen, the display card on the empty plinth states simply that the stone has been removed for cleaning,' said Holmes, 'and that is quite true; however, the full story is that it was actually removed several months ago.

'Last year it became apparent that considerable restoration work was required, work which would take a great deal of time. The Rosetta Stone is of course the museum's most famous exhibit, the one that attracts the most visitors. It was decided therefore that rather than leave the plinth empty for so long, the museum would, for the edification of the public and the information of the numerous scholars who come to study it, replace the stone with a replica.

'It was an excellent copy, if I may be allowed to say so, since I was involved in the initial study and the design. It is the same size and very nearly the same weight as the original, perfect in every detail, but there is a discreet marking on the copy, one which is hidden from general view by the frame of the protective case, which would immediately reveal its true nature. We thought this precaution to be essential as we did not wish to risk any possibility of such a fine copy to be mistaken for the real thing. We also ensured that any attempt to remove the marking would only make the nature of the artefact to be even more apparent.

'In the first week of January during that month's closure for cleaning, the Rosetta Stone was removed from the gallery and the copy installed in its place.'

I could see the astonishment on the faces of the delegates, apart, that is, from Bruno who merely looked puzzled at the others' reactions and had to be enlightened in French by Madame Dubois.

Professor Dümichen was clearly outraged by this news, so much so that for a moment he was speechless. 'Do you mean to tell us,' he said at last, 'that this copy, this false object, was displayed to the public and to scholars without so much as a note to say what its true nature was? That is a cheat, a fraud, a gross dishonesty. I must protest!'

'I agree with Professor Dümichen,' said Lepsius, more mildly. 'It seems to me that the museum has fallen from its usual high standards. I am only pleased that visitors are not charged a fee, or they might feel cheated, and you would be accused of fooling them in order to profit by it. It would not go well with the public to learn this. What of your trustees? Did they approve? And your government who pays so generous a grant?'

'That is a private matter,' said Dr Birch. 'We have broken no laws and acted only in the interests of preserving one of the most celebrated ancient artefacts in the country.'

Dümichen and Lepsius started talking to each other at once in what I took to be German, and it was left to Madame Dubois to break in.

'But might I ask,' she said in that polite yet firm tone which some ladies adopt when they do not expect to be rebuffed, 'if you have a copy of the stone, why is the plinth empty?'

'Yes! And where is it?' demanded Dümichen. 'The real one, I mean. I think we at least ought to be permitted to see it.'

'All in good time,' said Holmes, to Dümichen. 'And yes, Madame, that is an excellent question. Why is the plinth empty? That is because last week, when the museum was closed for its most recent cleaning some thieves broke in and stole the copy.'

There was a brief silence, then Lepsius said, 'I do not understand.'

Dümichen looked dumbfounded, while Bruno simply looked at the others in puzzlement, realising that something very unusual had been announced. Mme Dubois turned to Bruno and expressed this information in French. He muttered what were probably imprecations in his own language and made some elaborate gestures.

'Are you saying,' said Mme Dubois, 'that the copy has been taken by thieves who are under the impression they have the actual stone?'

'I think that is the case,' said Holmes.

Bruno asked something in French and Madame Dubois nodded. 'I must echo Dr Bruno's question,' she said. 'How was such a feat accomplished?'

'Have the police been advised? What are they doing?' asked Lepsius.

'The policed were called, and their investigations led them to inform us that the thieves employed equipment belonging to the museum to lift the stone from its plinth and transport it to the exit onto Montague Place. From there it was winched onto a hired wagon and carried away,' said Holmes. 'The police have surmised that it might have been taken to the area of the Docks and is concealed either on board a ship or in a warehouse. Large numbers of men have been employed to search all possible locations, but so far without result. The copy does of course have some intrinsic value and would be very much sought after by other museums so we would rather like to have it back.'

'There is another issue, of course,' said Birch. 'During the course of the robbery, two of our attendants were attacked, and one, a Mr Collier, died of his injuries. We are dealing with some very dangerous men.'

'How dreadful!' exclaimed Madame Dubois.

'But where is the stone?' asked Dümichen again. 'Why can we not see it?'

'I regret that the museum trustees have decreed that that information is not to be revealed, not to anyone,' said Holmes. 'The gang is thought to be a large one, and the museum is hard at work to ensure that its arrangements to preserve the safety of its collections are perfect and that such an outrage cannot therefore happen again. The police do have two men in custody, but they are both very minor criminals. Neither of them has been able to provide any useful information.'

In the general atmosphere of consternation, Madame Dubois explained the facts to Dr Bruno.

'I have one more question,' she said. 'Would the thieves not be able to see that the stone in their possession was a copy? You say there is a secret marking?'

'There is, but I am not about to disclose what it is,' said Holmes. 'I do not believe the thieves have the expertise to understand it, whereas to scholars of ancient Egypt such as yourselves, it would be quite obvious.'

The room briefly fell silent. If the delegates hoped that an exception might be made for them, they were to be disappointed.

Dr Birch cleared his throat. 'I will of course keep you informed as to any progress made,' he said. 'The police enquiries continue, and they remain hopeful of a resolution. Let us now move on to our examination of the Saqqara fragments.'

The meeting continued and considering my lack of interest in the misshapen pieces of stone under discussion it was all I could do to appear to be fascinated by the debate. But I did manage some commendably tidy notes which I turned over to Dr Birch at the end of the meeting.

'You will have observed,' said Holmes as we discussed developments with Birch and Martinson later on, 'that the installation of the copy was supposed to have taken place at the beginning of January, two weeks before the start of the Castellani exhibition, in other words shortly before Collier was engaged, thus explaining why he knew nothing of it.'

'Do you really believe that one of the delegates has something to do with this?' asked Dr Birch.

'I do,' he said.

I never dared ask Holmes which of the delegates he suspected. His only comment on that subject was that he believed the status of delegate gave the criminal the best opportunity to ask searching questions and receive explanations that would never have been given to a member of the public. But I thought I knew. I had seen Holmes' ears prick up like a startled deer at my description of Professor Dümichen. From that moment on, the stupendously intelligent adversary achieved a physical form in his mind, as a man with an enormously domed white cranium who became, for him, the archetype of the evil genius. I sometimes wondered if he exaggerated this feature when he described the men who he believed to be his ultimate enemies.

'What do you plan to do now?' I asked.

'You recall that during the initial incursion into the museum the keys which Attendant Finley carried were stolen,' said Holmes. 'Those keys were never recovered, and I believe that Collier passed them to his associates to enable them to unlock the door leading to the basement, which had already been determined as the hiding place. The museum had the outer locks changed and new keys made, but no-one thought to replace the basement key and lock, as it was never imagined at the time that the criminals had gone down there.'

Martinson sighed. 'A terrible oversight, I know.'

'Does that mean the gang still has the key to the basement?' I exclaimed.

'I will see to it that the lock is changed at once,' said Birch.

'All in good time,' said Holmes with a smile. 'But not just yet. That oversight will play to our advantage.'

CHAPTER TWENTY-EIGHT

Holmes' plan as he outlined it to us was an adventurous one, possibly even a dangerous one, but a plan that could only be entrusted to a very few persons. One of those was Sergeant Lestrade, who was summoned to the museum by urgent message. On Holmes' advice Dr Birch and Dr Martinson prepared the ground, but they would not join the three of us, as we lay in wait for our quarry.

The museum was still crowded with visitors, and we had nothing to fear for some time, but as dusk approached, we suspected that our man would make his move. As the galleries emptied of visitors, we ventured underground. Mindful of the prospect of violence, Holmes had armed himself with a singlestick. He used it in his practice as a swordsman and I had no doubt that he was extremely adept in its use. I had no weapons, and although my shoulder was almost as good as new, I was dubious as to what assistance I might be able to provide.

Once again, the tiny flame of Holmes' pocket lantern illuminated the way down the steps of the museum's basement storeroom. The odour emitted by the lantern was only slight compared to one of the usual size, which was fortunate since we did not want to give an intruder any warning that he was expected. We felt sure, however, that he would be obliged to bring a personal source of light, whose odour would more than obscure that of ours. Once we were inside, the upper door was locked. Only someone with a key would be able to enter.

When we reached the storerooms, Holmes, in his intent methodical way, made sure to examine the floor very closely. I had no doubt that he had committed every detail of it to memory in order to compare it to our last visit. Sergeant Lestrade looked about him, bemused by the crowded room of ancient treasures. He was unsure, as I was too, to some extent, about what he might be required to do, but I was pleased to see that a stout truncheon and a set of handcuffs were a prominent part of his equipment.

At length Holmes gave a sigh of satisfaction. 'I can confirm that no-one has been in here since we made our discovery. Whoever it is we are expecting he would not have thought anything was amiss with his scheme until this afternoon, and he has not yet had the opportunity to examine the stone.'

'Are you sure that an attempt will be made this afternoon?' I asked.

'The delegates are leaving tomorrow,' said Holmes. 'I am convinced that the criminal we seek will not be able to resist coming down here to check on the veracity of my statement. This is his last opportunity. He must choose his moment, when the attendants are ushering the crowds from the museum, and he will not be observed slipping away for a few minutes. Dr Birch has given special orders to the attendants to made it possible for him to have a clear chance of coming here. If the door to the basement was guarded, or the gallery still occupied, he would not be able make an attempt and the chance of capture would be lost.'

'Will he not suspect a trap?' I asked.

'He will, but the consequences of his ignoring the bait and being wrong mean that he will take the risk. We have lured him in, but this may not be enough. If he is, as I believe, a member of the delegation, then he might easily excuse his presence here by claiming scholarly curiosity, which will be impossible to disprove, and our efforts will be lost. We must be certain of him. Once he reveals that he knows where the stone is hidden, we have him.'

'I hope it will not be a long wait,' I said. I was already shivering a little because the room was cold, and possibly also due to a quite natural nervousness.

We progressed through to the second room, where, due to the jutting shelves laden with statuary and bulbous vases, there was better concealment. Lestrade was able to blend into a shadowy corner, and I did my best to appear invisible. We unrolled some of the museum's wrapping cloths onto the floor and there made as good a seating as possible.

'I am sorry not to have brought a pack of cards for amusement,' said Holmes. 'But in any case, I am about to cover the light. Gentlemen, once I have done so, we must remain as quiet as possible, and be alert to whatever transpires. Once discovered he may try to make a swift escape, which I hope to prevent.'

Holmes, his singlestick by his side and ready to hand, lowered the metal cover of the lantern, concealing the little flame, and plunging us into darkness. And there we were, enclosed in our tomb, locked in, and I for one began to have fears that through some fault we would unexpectedly find ourselves unable to leave, and would be forgotten there, without food or water, driven to madness and a cruel death. It was a gruesome thought. Holmes was utterly calm. As my eyes became used to the faint light from the upper vents, I saw him in profile, that noble beak of a nose, the firm determined mouth, the intelligent brow, leaning his head against the wall.

We cannot have been waiting for long when there was a faint noise, what I judged to be that of a key turning in the lock at the top of the stairs. The door opened very carefully, and footsteps sounded, indicating that someone had entered. There was a pause, then the closing of the door. Whoever it was did not re-lock it, a precaution, perhaps to ensure that a rapid departure was possible. We hardly dared to breathe. I could feel my heart surging in my chest, and the beating was so loud in my ears that I feared the intruder would be able to hear it. There was a faint scraping sound from above, and the hissing flare of a match. Gradually, soft footsteps descended, and there was an odd echo in the darkness of our venerable dungeon, almost as if two sets of feet were moving in unison. A yellow light was thrown upon the wall of the first room, its movement suggesting the flicker of a candle. I was at that moment very pleased that Dr Martinson was not of our number.

I glanced at Holmes, and he was leaning forward, his nostrils twitching like a hound scenting his quarry and ready for the hunt. Slowly, soundlessly, he rose to his feet, making sure to remain concealed behind the projecting shelves, his singlestick held down at his side. He laid a finger to his lips, and beckoned me to stand, which I did very carefully, gently rotating my stiff shoulder, but ready to assist.

We had chosen to conceal ourselves slightly deeper in the storeroom from the place where the stone was concealed, to give us the best position from which to confront the intruder. Lestrade was guarding the other side of the room, closer to the entrance. The footsteps approached, and a halo of light formed. We shrank back a little to make the best of our hiding places for as long as possible. We knew that a figure had entered the room, advancing by the light of a candle.

What would have transpired next, I do not know, but Holmes chose his moment, and emerged rapidly from the concealment of the shelves to make the confrontation. I made to join him, which may seem to have been an act of reckless courage on my part, but in an odd way it was pure cowardice as I felt that the nearer I was to Holmes, the safer I was likely to be. He, however, motioned me to remain where I was, and I complied. It is a well-known phenomenon that lighting a human face from below creates shadows and highlights which give it an evil, even supernatural appearance, and even though I was familiar with this effect, seeing such an apparition before me in that gloomy room was a horrible shock. This was not however my greatest shock, since the pale countenance before me was that of Madame Dubois.

Holmes too was surprised. He was about to speak when Madame Dubois, her features contracted with apprehension, yet bravely holding on to her nerve, gasped out, 'Take care! He has a gun!'

'Indeed, I do,' said a voice behind her. It was a man's voice and not one I had heard before. 'And it is loaded and pointing at Madame Dubois. But it can just as easily be trained on anyone else who might be here, and I am unafraid to use it. Now then, I suggest that you remain quite still, while she carries out the task I have set for her.'

'I will not prevent it,' said Holmes.

'I must assume from your presence that you know where the item is to be found,' said the voice.

'It would be futile to deny it.'

'Mr Holmes, I recognise your voice,' said Madame Dubois. 'Kindly tell me what I am to look for.'

'I can, but you might not be able to reach it unassisted.'

'Really, Mr Holmes,' she said tersely, 'I have excavated Egyptian tombs, I think I can search a storeroom.'

There was a slight intake of breath from Holmes. 'Yes, of course. Please place your candle on the shelf immediately to your right. I have a lantern and will direct its light where you need to go.'

'Oh, do not trouble yourself,' said the voice. 'I think I can recognise when a game has been played. This was all a trick to entrap me. The stone is the stone, and our day is done. There is no copy, no secret marking. And now it only remains for me to leave you. No-one must make a move. I will depart and lock you in here. Anyone who tries to prevent me will be shot.'

The utter simplicity with which he made that statement was terrifying. I was convinced that if he felt it to be necessary, he would be the only person to leave the basement alive. The thoughts that rushed through my mind at that moment were a determination to do something followed by a sense of helplessness at not knowing what to do. Madame Dubois had obeyed Holmes' request, and stepped closer to the shelves, and I felt sure that the gun would now be trained on him as the greater threat. It then occurred to me that the man was still unaware of my presence, and that if I took care I could move in silence. I stretched out my arm, and my fingertips touched a statuette on the edge of a shelf. I gave it a push and it fell to the stone floor with a clatter.

It was in that moment, with the gunman momentarily startled by the noise, and the lady no longer in the line of fire, that Holmes acted. The villain must have thought himself safe from attack, out of arm's reach, but he had not bargained for the singlestick or the strength and lightning power with which it could be used. In what must have been a movement faster than any eye could see, Holmes, standing his ground, lashed out and the tip of the singlestick struck the gunman's wrist with a sound like the cracking of bone. There was a cry, and a gunshot, very loud, echoed in the crowded room, with a splintering crash and a muffled gasp from Madame Dubois. Then another shape hurtled out of the shadows, and two solid forms collided. All was confusion for a time, with the sound of grunts and scuffling, gasps and muttered oaths, and finally a metallic clink.

At last, the little pocket lantern and Madame Dubois' candle were allowed to cast their light on the scene. Both Holmes and the lady appeared unharmed.

'Is anyone hurt?' I asked.

'No, and we must thank Sergeant Lestrade for his swift response,' said Holmes. 'He has knocked the gun far from the criminal's reach and secured him. But there is a rather splendid amphora here which will need extensive restoration.' He bowed to Madame Dubois. 'My apologies for unwittingly exposing you to such dangers. If I had known that you might be here, I would have acted differently.'

'No apologies are necessary,' she said. 'It is I who must thank you. As you will have guessed, this person, whoever he may be, waylaid me and threatened me with his gun, requiring me to carry out his scheme.'

Holmes turned the lantern to the figures on the floor, where Lestrade, kneeling on the back of his prisoner, had secured the handcuffs. 'Now then, sir,' said Lestrade to the man lying prostrate beneath him, 'it won't do to struggle. I can always make the darbies tighter if you want. And don't try and run away, because there are constables at every door.'

'What a cowardly fellow,' said Holmes, contemptuously.

'And he is no more Italian than I am,' said Madame Dubois, as the man we had known as Dr Bruno revealed a detailed acquaintance with some of the riper English expletives.

'Now then, you cur, silence your language, there is a lady present,' said Holmes, 'or I might be obliged to close your foul mouth for you.'

'I think when we get him into the light, we will find his true origins are more nearly in the region of Mayfair,' said Lestrade.

'If I'm not mistaken, his name is Samuel Nokes. English father, mother of French extraction. Clever type. Good start in life but then went wrong. He runs some of the most brutal criminal gangs in London. We have been trying to get our hands on him for some time.'

The sound of gunfire had alerted some attention by now, and Lestrade's constables came as fast as they could, lantern-lit down the stairs, to assist him in removing the snarling gang-leader to the police station.

'I assume,' said Holmes to Madame Dubois, 'that the task assigned to you by that villain was to examine the Rosetta Stone to establish that it was, as I had stated, simply a copy.'

'It was. He told me at first that he had found the stolen copy and wanted my opinion. When I suggested advising the museum, he prevented me by drawing a gun. I already knew that your story was false and realised that it must be a trick to force the criminal to reveal himself, and that you suspected one of us.'

'How did you recognise the trick?' asked Holmes.

She gave a little laugh. 'I came to London last month to see the Castellani collection, and while I was here, I made sure to pay a visit to an old friend — the Rosetta Stone. Had it been a copy I would have known it then. But I suspected Bruno even before he pulled the gun from his pocket. Had he been a true scholar, he would not have needed me to examine the stone for him.'

CHAPTER TWENTY-NINE

Holmes, who despite his often-expressed disdain for the female sex, could be quite the gallant when a gallant was required, and he conducted Madame Dubois up the gloomy stairs to the gallery where Dr Birch and Dr Martinson were anxiously waiting.

'Edith!' gasped Martinson. 'Please reassure me that you are uninjured!'

Madame Dubois smiled. 'No harm is done,' she said, gently. After a brief hesitation she offered her hand to him and he, after matching her hesitation, capitulated and took the tips of her fingers in his.

Dr Birch soon established that we were all whole, and required nothing more than a stimulating beverage, which he was happy to supply. Dr Martinson and Madame Dubois, after their pure and modest intimate moment, were silent as they sipped from glasses of water, but exchanged frequent glances, and it was unclear as to which one of the two blushed more than the other. Hearty congratulations were in order, and Holmes, who was kind enough to thank me for my trivial part in the capture, made sure to praise Sergeant Lestrade who he said more than made up in firmness of action what he lacked in intuition.

Dr Birch was content that the whole incident was now settled and that the Rosetta Stone could be restored to its usual place. Holmes agreed, and while he said no more on the subject, I could see that he was still troubled.

As we left the museum, I commented on how pleased I was that Dr Martinson and Madame Dubois were finally on friendly terms.

'There is still an obstacle to their union,' said Holmes. 'You may be interested to know that I have uncovered some further details of the fire that killed George Luckhurst's parents. Madame Dubois was able to provide me with sufficient information of place and date which enabled me to find the inquest report in the newspapers. There were only four persons in the house at the time, Luckhurst's parents, Martinson and the servant Greenleaf. It is fortunate that the other servants did not sleep in the house or there might have been greater loss of life. The fire was started by a fallen oil lamp. The Luckhursts had retired for the night, but Martinson was still about and stated that he believed he must have fallen asleep downstairs. He awoke to find the house on fire. Greenleaf testified that he was making his rounds to see that the house was in order before retiring to his room, when Mrs Luckhurst's pet puppy dog jumped up and knocked over the lamp. The house was ablaze before he could take any action, and he was obliged to leap from a window to save himself. In doing so he broke his leg and was unable to provide any assistance in saving the family. The inquest returned a verdict of accidental death.'

'It does not seem that anyone can be held to blame,' I said.

'So it appeared. However, a correspondent later wrote to *The Times* with some very pointed observations. He felt that too much freedom and pampering was given to household pets which he said should never be allowed to roam unguarded for fear of accident as they can be impossible to discipline. He appears to have known the Luckhursts, and commented with some irony that the dog, while the guilty party, was the only occupant of the house to escape unscathed, since it was later discovered outside the house by neighbours who took it in and found that its fur was not so much as singed.'

'That is remarkable,' I said.

'Very,' said Holmes. 'Indeed, I find the incident of the dog quite curious.'

'Oh?'

'It leads me to wonder if the dog was after all the cause of the fire. If innocent, it has been blamed for another's negligence.'

'Do you think Greenleaf might have caused the fire by accident?' I asked.

'The fact is,' said Holmes, 'that either he or Martinson might have done so. But taking into account Martinson's expressions of guilt, his sudden abjuration of alcohol and devoted care of his nephew suggests either that he was the cause, or he thinks he was. If he was under the influence of alcohol that night, as seems probable, since he had fallen asleep downstairs, he might not know for certain. Greenleaf's story of the dog knocking over the lamp was likely an invention, to protect either himself or his master. And I very much doubt that the truth of the matter has ever been the subject of conversation between the two. Each man has locked it inside himself.'

'Madame Dubois appears to be generous and kind. If Dr Martinson confessed to her, she might forgive him.'

'She might, but he will never forgive himself.'

'It is a delicate situation,' I said.

'It is,' agreed Holmes, 'and I believe I have taken logical deduction as far as it will go. But Madame Dubois is an exceptional lady, and I think she has a higher degree of that instinct with which women are naturally endowed. We will see what transpires.'

CHAPTER THIRTY

On the final day of the delegates' visit to the museum, there was a small convivial gathering in Dr Birch's apartments, to which Holmes and I were cordially invited.

'We have received some excellent news,' said Dr Birch. 'Mr Finley, released from police custody without a stain on his character, has been pronounced well enough to return to his duties next week. He has always been an exemplary employee. When he was told about Collier's infamy, he recalled that Collier had once asked to borrow his keys and he had quite rightly refused, saying that they must never leave his person. We now think that Collier was planning to make an impression so copies could be made. When that plan failed, he was obliged to resort to violence.'

'I have heard from Sergeant Lestrade, who tells me that Mr Nokes will soon be appearing before the magistrates on a number of extremely serious charges, and will almost certainly be sent for trial,' said Martinson. 'He will not be seeing the light of day for some very considerable time.'

Holmes was content to accept the praise of the gathering, although I believe he was troubled by the thought that Nokes was not the commander-in-chief but simply a lieutenant.

'That will be a feather in the sergeant's cap, I imagine,' said Birch, 'and the inspector's too. Although I fear that Mr Holmes' part in this will remain obscure for the time being.'

'Ah Mr Holmes,' sighed Martinson, 'I wish you could solve ancient mysteries as well as you do those of today.'

'I do not have your years of expertise in Egyptian history and customs,' said Holmes.

'Even so, would you humour us a little?'

'By all means.'

Dr Birch poured fresh libations of sherry and water, and Dr Martinson proceeded to explain.

'It ought to be a simple matter, but it is not. The location and construction of the tomb tells us without any doubt that it dates from what is commonly known as the Old Kingdom. It was a somewhat mysterious period, in fact rather chaotic at times. Even with the wonderful list of Seti I —' Martinson gave a respectful nod to Professor Dümichen — 'we are still assembling our history of the early dynasties. Some pharaohs only reigned for a short while. At least one we believe to have been murdered by the pharaoh who succeeded him. But they were, we understand from the available records, all buried in the necropolis of Saqqara, the pyramids of which have yet to be fully explored. Seti I reigned much later, in the nineteenth dynasty. His list includes all those who he deemed to be lawful pharaohs. The few monuments and papyri we have confirm the legitimacy of the pharaohs in the list. That being the case there is no reason we can see why this individual, who had started to build his own royal tomb, should have been erased.'

'And you say that even the pharaoh who murdered his predecessor was considered to be a legitimate ruler?' asked Holmes.

'All the material we have discovered so far suggests that,' said Dr Birch. 'However, we have established that the tomb we are studying is not his. The fragments we have of the broken cartouches while not revealing a name does indicate from a partial hieroglyph that it must have been that of another.'

'Might it have been a tomb constructed for one of the other pharaohs which was abandoned before completion? Perhaps because the structure was not sound?' asked Holmes.

'We did consider that,' said Lepsius. 'This tomb was not well built. The construction appeared hurried, badly done, by excavators with limited skills. I agree that tombs were sometimes abandoned only partly constructed where there were obvious faults, but had that been the case here, the cartouches, the inscriptions, would have been preserved, not destroyed. The cartouche is a protection, a sign of royalty. No, there is only one conclusion. This pharaoh's name is never to be spoken. Our eyes were not to light upon it, for fear that he would rise and live again.'

'And whoever was destined for the tomb, it would have been commenced during his lifetime, in fact quite early in his reign?' said Holmes.

'Yes, it would.'

'Or even before?'

'I would not deny that possibility. A prince or princess would expect to be interred in a royal tomb. But that does not explain the erasure.'

'But a usurper,' said Holmes, 'someone not entitled to ascend the throne, a natural son without royal status, or not of royal blood at all, but planning to become Pharaoh by assassination? Would such an individual have been erased from history if his treacherous plans were detected before he was able to carry them out?'

Dümichen and Lepsius glanced at each other. 'That would be the ultimate punishment,' said Lepsius, 'so, yes.'

'Mr Holmes, are you suggesting that this individual began the construction of a royal tomb, not because he was actually royal but because he anticipated that by assassination he would become so?' asked Madame Dubois.

'That is my suggestion,' said Holmes.

The members of the delegation, Dr Birch and Dr Martinson all fell silent. There were several moments of academic rumination.

'There are a number of possibilities,' said Dr Birch, at last. At this point he was at once assailed by names being put forward by the other experts, all of them speaking at once and then bursting in to evaluate the suggestions of the others. From what I could gather it appeared that Pharaohs often had several wives, and a plethora of mistresses, and it was a hard task even at the time to determine how many offspring they had. Animated as the discussion was, I felt assured that given the friendly terms of the participants, it would not descend into a squabble.

'I am sure this will be a fruitful exchange of opinion,' Holmes observed to me.

'I can see many years of work and numerous controversial publications,' I said, 'if they ever reach a conclusion, that is. I only wonder that they never thought of it.'

'I expect they did not read the Donaldson case,' said Holmes.

By now, Birch and Martinson were pulling books down from shelves and unrolling documents across the desk while the others gathered around to view them, and Holmes and I decided to thank our host and depart.

CHAPTER THIRTY-ONE

Samuel Nokes, we later discovered, was the son of a well-born army man who had against the wishes of his family, contracted a marriage with an actress of French extraction. Initially the son had enjoyed a good education. By the time the boy was eighteen, however, his father had dissipated his fortune at the gaming tables and sought solace in the brandy bottle, and his mother returned to her former profession. Nokes, equipped with an excellent memory, a talent for impersonation and some facility with the language of his mother, had drifted into crime. He often masqueraded as a foreign nobleman in order to relieve unsuspecting victims of their funds and was easily able to command men of lesser intellect.

Nokes had realised that he would not be able to disguise himself as a native-born Frenchman in the company of Madame Dubois. He had made sufficient preparation for the scheme, however, to adopt the persona of an Italian who spoke a little French. Claiming some familiarity with the exhibits at Turin he had inveigled himself into the delegation while it was on its way to London, learning all the while from conversation in English that he was not believed to have understood. Any deficits in his knowledge had been ascribed to differences in language.

When questioned by the police Nokes agreed only those facts which he could not deny and were already known. Henry Collier, he confirmed, had been a useful young rascal, whom he engaged on encountering him at the London Regent Hotel.

When asked for the names of the other men in his gang, however, he declared that he did no more than hire and pay them and did not trouble himself to learn their names. He denied that he worked for anyone else.

I commented to Holmes that a long prison sentence was inevitable. Holmes observed drily that whatever the outcome, he doubted that we had heard the last of Samuel Nokes. His prediction was borne out not long afterwards, when Nokes escaped from custody in a disguise smuggled to him by a confederate. Inspector Caldwell, who had been hoping for a promotion following the capture of such a notorious criminal and instead earned a severe reprimand for negligence, was particularly unhappy at this development.

Perfect secrecy is rarely possible, and one of the more sensational newspapers must have loosened the tongue of an informant. It published a story announcing that the Rosetta Stone had been stolen, elaborating the theme by stating confidently that the famous treasure was already on a ship bound for Egypt, and a bloody conflict was therefore inevitable. On the same day, however, anxious visitors flooding the museum found the stone back in its accustomed place, and the attendants roundly denying any truth in the rumour. The newspaper did not publish an apology for the falsified story, but then the papers rarely did.

Holmes did admit to me later that he had been briefly distracted by the unusual appearance of Professor Dümichen. He was aware from the article in *The Illustrated London News* that both Dümichen and Lepsius had visited the museum in 1874, and were known to Dr Birch and Dr Martinson, however this did not in his eyes absolve either of them from being criminal masterminds.

The profession of Egyptologist was in itself a perfect means of concealing an individual's baser principles, while conferring privilege and respect. He confessed, however, that on this occasion he had been wrong, and both the visiting professors were innocent of any wrongdoing.

'Everyone blunders from time to time, Stamford. The secret is to recognise and learn from one's blunders. They are a necessary curb to arrogance and overconfidence.'

Holmes did however have some very welcome news. 'It appears,' he said, 'that following my conversation with Madame Dubois her astute intuition has guided her and certain matters have been resolved. She conducted a private conversation with Mr Greenleaf, and he was persuaded to throw some light on the reasons for Dr Martinson's unhappiness. She has not divulged what was said, and it was not my place to ask. I am pleased to say that she now intends to remain in London where she has been engaged to make drawings for the museum. We will of course never discover how the tragic fire came about; however, I am told that Mr Greenleaf has decided to retire from service. He has some small savings which will provide a pension and intends to go and live quietly with a married sister in Sussex. She keeps bees.'

I had some good news of my own. I had remained in touch with George Luckhurst who wrote to me saying that following the death of his great-aunt he had inherited an annuity, which would greatly further his career. He intended, once he had completed his final examinations, to spend some weeks in Greece, and invited me to travel with him. The prospect of summer sun, good food and wine, and an education in classical art was very appealing and I accepted.

I had imagined that the adventure of the Rosetta Stone was simply one of those remarkable incidents which would come along only once in a lifetime. How wrong I was. Anyone who Sherlock Holmes took into his confidence was destined to be swept up from time to time into the strangest of circumstances, and this mysterious case would not be the last that Holmes and I were to investigate.

HISTORICAL NOTES

The Rosetta Stone

The Rosetta Stone is carved with a decree dating from 196 BCE, in three versions, Ancient Egyptian hieroglyphs and demotic script, and Ancient Greek. It was discovered in 1799 and at once aroused considerable interest because of its potential to unlock the mystery of the hieroglyphs. It was brought to London in 1801 and first displayed at the British Museum in 1802. The hieroglyphs were deciphered by French scholar Jean-François Champollion (1790–1832) whose studies were first published in 1822. Its name has become synonymous with the concept of a key to decryption and the solution of mysteries.

The stone, which had been given a protective coating of wax by the museum, was once believed to be composed of black basalt, and is so described in the nineteenth-century guidebooks. Only when the stone was cleaned in 1999 was its material identified as dark grey granodiorite.

The stone on its plinth, held in its purpose-built cradle and covered in a protective frame, can be seen on page 9 of *The Illustrated London News* 26 September 1874. Nowadays it is displayed in a glass case. It remains one of the most popular exhibits in the museum.

The British Museum

https://www.britishmuseum.org

The first British Museum was in Montague House, where collections were opened to the public in 1759. The current building is on the site of the demolished Montague House. It was constructed over a number of years and completed in

1852. It housed collections of antiquities, natural history and The King's Library. By 1876 when this book is set, the expanding collections meant that it was becoming seriously overcrowded. Keepers of the antiquities often expressed their frustration at the space taken up by the natural history exhibits, especially the whales, and the fact that so many treasures were consigned to the basement which was not suitable for the public to visit. The natural history collections were removed to the newly built Museum of Natural History in 1887.

Initially the museum was lit only by daylight because of fear of fire, which greatly restricted the hours of opening. Electric lighting was installed in 1890.

The museum closed for three separate weeks each year for regular cleaning. It was closed for this purpose in the first week of May 1876.

The description of the basement storeroom, which was not open to the public, is from the imagination of the author. Similarly, with the workshop. I have not been able to find precise descriptions of how large exhibits were moved but have made assumptions based on general practices and the equipment available at the time. Any errors in these areas are solely those of the author.

I am greatly indebted to the online collection of out of copyright material, archive.org, a veritable treasure trove for the researcher, which provided me with contemporary catalogues and visitors' guidebooks of the British Museum, and guides for travellers to Egypt. I have also made extensive use of contemporary newspapers and information and images on the British Museum website. I am very sorry that I was unable to visit the museum during the writing of this book due to the Coronavirus pandemic.

The keepers of the British Museum are the department heads. In 1876 antiquarian and Egyptologist Dr Samuel Birch (1813–1885) was Keeper of Oriental Antiquities. His early studies were of Chinese and he translated a number of Chinese works.

The museum employed senior and junior keepers and senior assistants who were qualified academics. Senior keepers and their families lived in apartments in the accommodation wings.

In January 1876 the museum announced a special exhibition of the valuable Castellani collection, which included gold jewellery, which was displayed for about two months.

One of the worst cases of vandalism in the museum was the shattering of the Portland Vase, a Roman glass exhibit in 1845 by a drunken visitor. It has been restored several times since.

On 1 August 1876 the museum was voted its annual grant from Parliament of £80,477.

Karl Richard Lepsius (1810–1884) was an extensively published Prussian Egyptologist.

Johannes Dümichen (1833–1894) was professor of Egyptology in Strasbourg. There is a splendid picture of him here:
https://en.wikipedia.org/wiki/Johannes_Dümichen

Details of the Abydos King List may be seen here:
https://en.wikipedia.org/wiki/Abydos_King_List

The Saqqara fragment and the tomb it came from are fictional.

In 1876 Bloomsbury inquests were held at The King's Head Tavern, Broad Street. The tavern was later demolished, and Broad Street absorbed into High Holborn.

Holmes uses his pocket lantern in *The Sign of Four* and *The Adventure of Wisteria Lodge*.

Bickford fuse was a safety fuse invented by William Bickford in 1831, intended to make the ignition of blasting charges safer. It burns at the rate of 1 foot in 30 seconds. It was widely used in the mining industry.

I am greatly indebted to Stephen Miller, Chartered Explosives Engineer, for his advice concerning the smoke device, its construction, use and behaviour. This is not, of course, something to be attempted by the reader!

The facts of the fictional Donaldson murder are loosely based on the 1905 crimes of Arthur Devereux. See the author's *Greater London Murders* (The History Press, 2012).

When Holmes described the horrible murder in a peaceful country village in chapter twenty-two, he must have been thinking of the Denham Massacre of 1870.

A NOTE TO THE READER

The timeline of the events in the life of Sherlock Holmes in the canonical fifty-six stories and four novels has occupied, fascinated and sometimes frustrated Holmesian scholars for many years. The most commonly accepted year of Holmes' birth is 1854. He did not meet Dr Watson and occupy 221b Baker Street before 1881.

Almost nothing is known about his early life and very little about his education. I think it is possible that, like Conan Doyle, he spent a year at school on the continent, where he acquired his knowledge of modern languages. He is known to have spent two years at a collegiate university, which means either Oxford or Cambridge, although which one, and what courses he took have never been revealed, but he did not take a degree. The year in which he settled permanently in London is unspecified. His first recorded case is that of the *Gloria Scott*, as recounted to Dr Watson, which took place during the university vacation. Holmes had been developing his powers of observation and deduction and was known amongst fellow students for his singular method of analysing problems. At the time this was nothing more to him than an intellectual exercise. During his work on the *Gloria Scott* mystery, however, it was suggested to him that he would make a brilliant detective and that idea took hold and gave him a direction in life.

Holmes realised that he lacked the broad and varied fields of knowledge which would serve as a foundation for his mental skills. The next few years were dedicated to acquiring that knowledge, and in doing so, he created the man who burst upon the literary scene and met Dr Watson in the first Holmes novel, *A Study in Scarlet*.

In my work, I have suggested that Holmes was at university during the years 1873–75, solving the *Gloria Scott* mystery after his second year. Realising that his particular requirements could not be provided by a university course, he did not return, choosing instead to undertake his own studies. He had boxed and fenced at university and while there is no evidence that he devoted dedicated practice to either later on, it is clear that these were skills he retained. His lodgings in London's Montague Street placed him close to the British Museum where he must have spent many hours studying in the library, and he enrolled at St Bartholomew's Medical College for practical courses in chemistry and anatomy.

And that is where my story begins.

Reviews are so important to authors, and if you enjoyed the novel I would be grateful if you could spare a few minutes to post a review on **Amazon** and **Goodreads**. I love hearing from readers, and you can connect with me online, **on Facebook**, **Twitter**, and **Instagram**.

You can also stay up to date with all my news via **my website** and by signing up to **my newsletter**.

Linda Stratmann

2021

lindastratmann.com

234

Sapere Books is an exciting new publisher of brilliant fiction and popular history.

To find out more about our latest releases and our monthly bargain books visit our website:
saperebooks.com

Printed in Great Britain
by Amazon

22009149R00136